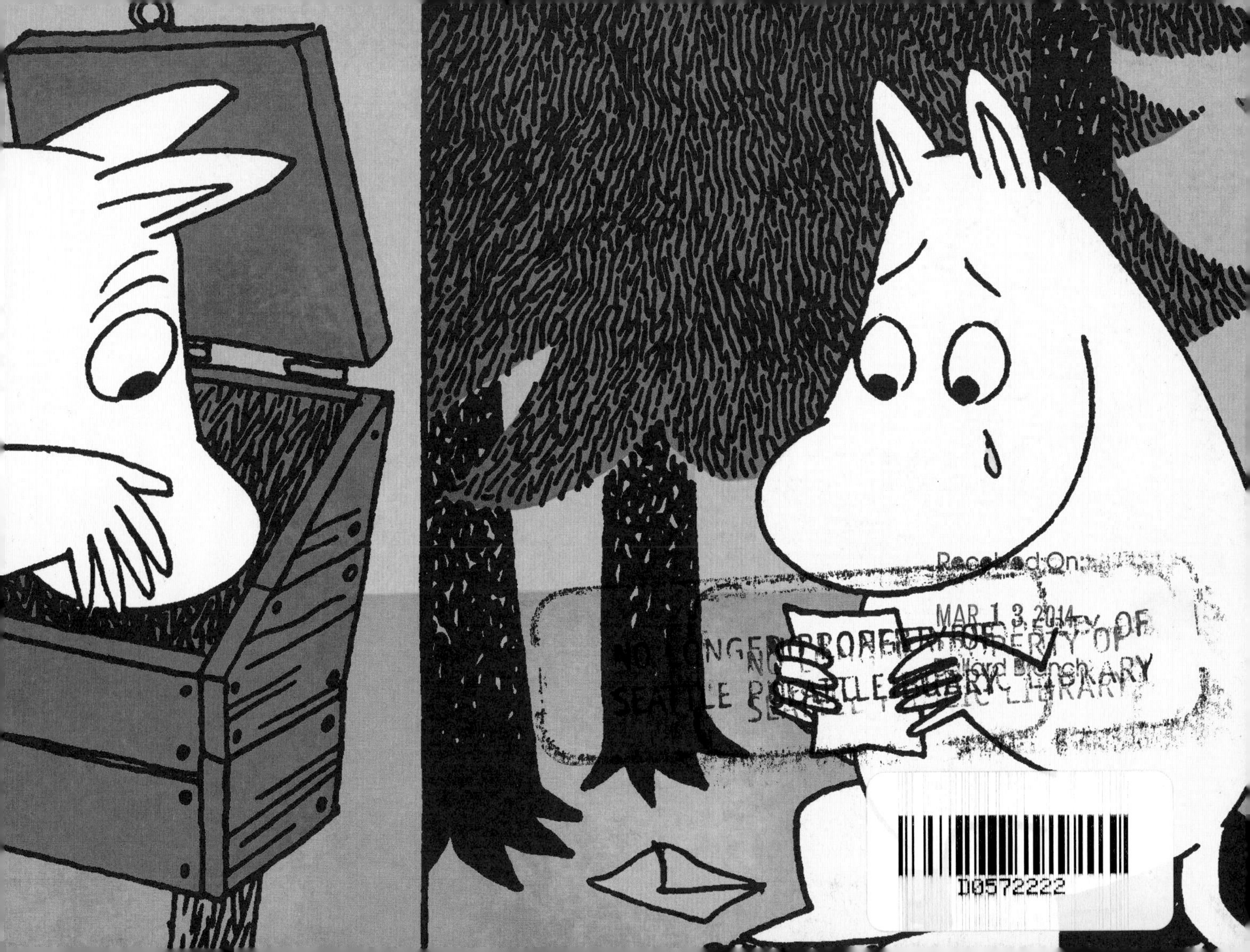

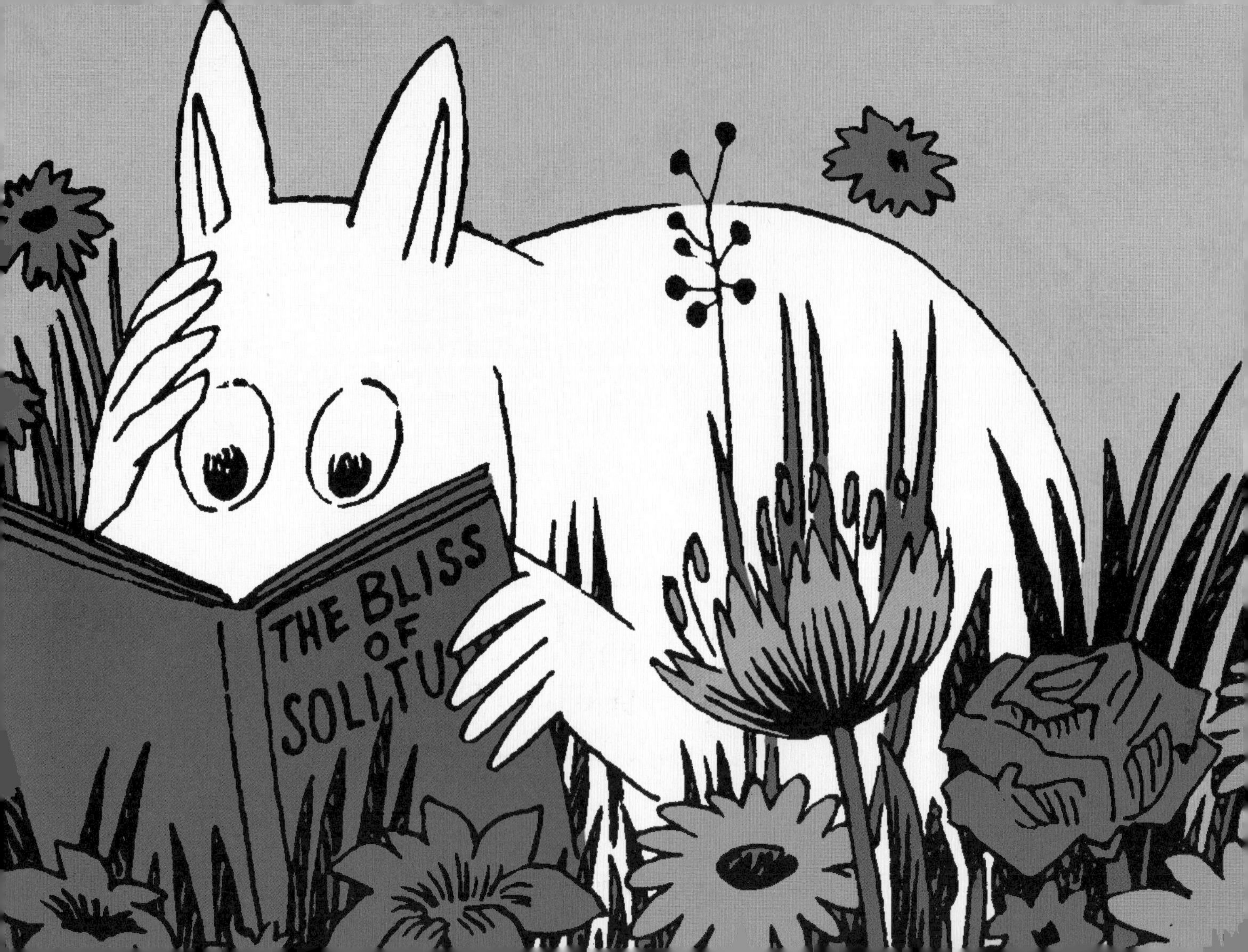
THE BLISS OF SOLITU

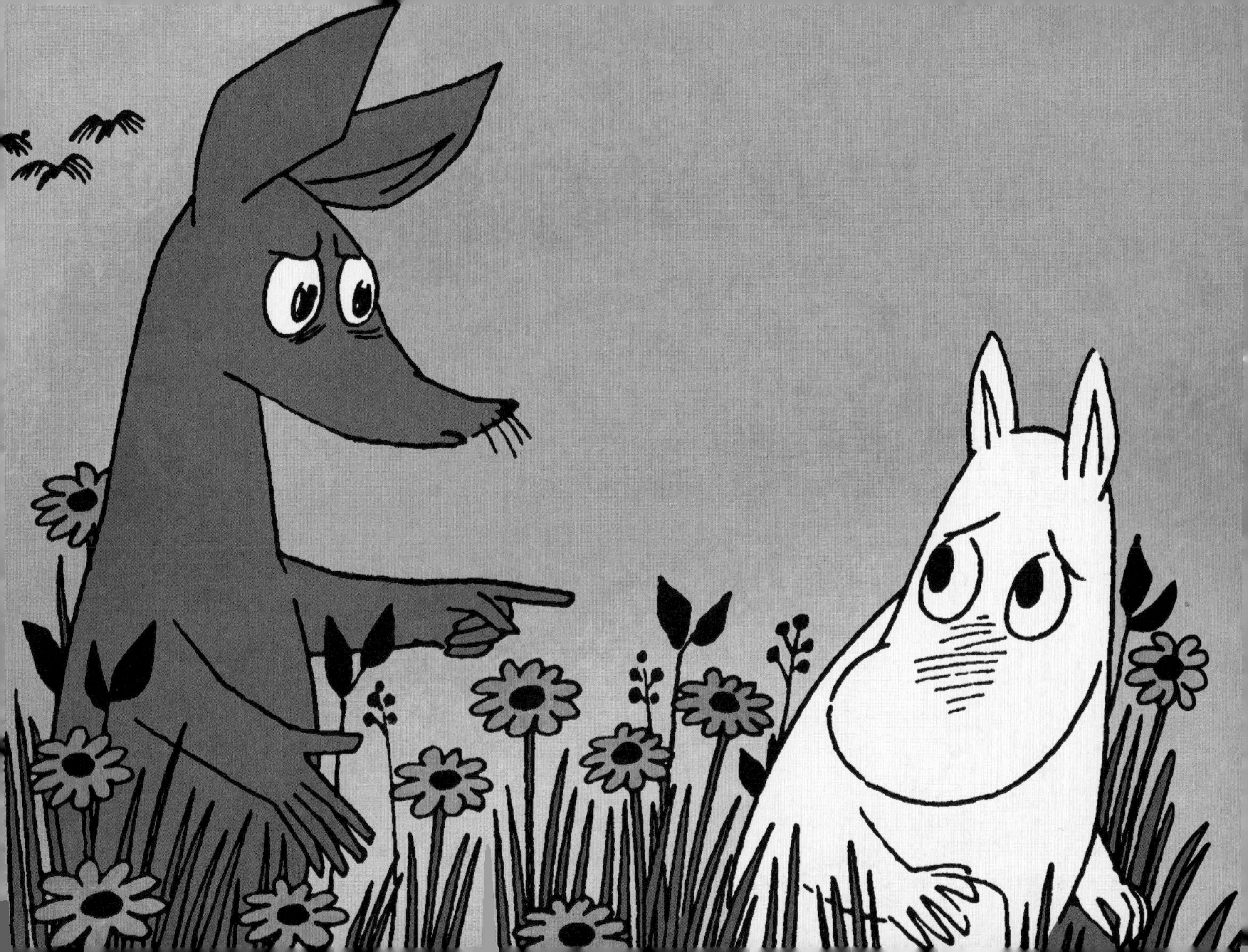

Enfant is an imprint of Drawn & Quarterly.

www.drawnandquarterly.com

First edition: January 2014
Printed in Malaysia
10 9 8 7 6 5 4 3 2 1

Library and Archives Canada Cataloguing in Publication
Jansson, Tove, artist
Moomin and the Golden Tail / Tove Jansson.
Originally published in Evening news, London, [1958].
ISBN 978-1-77046-133-8 (pbk.)
1. Graphic novels. I. Title.
PZ7.7.J35Moa 2013   j741.5'94897
C2013-902363-1

Published in the USA by Enfant, a client publisher of
Farrar, Straus and Giroux
Orders: 888.330.8477

Published in Canada by Enfant, a client publisher of
Raincoast Books
Orders: 800.663.5714

Distributed in the United Kingdom by
Publishers Group UK
Orders: info@pguk.co.uk

MOOMIN AND THE GOLDEN TAIL

Tove Jansson

ENFANT

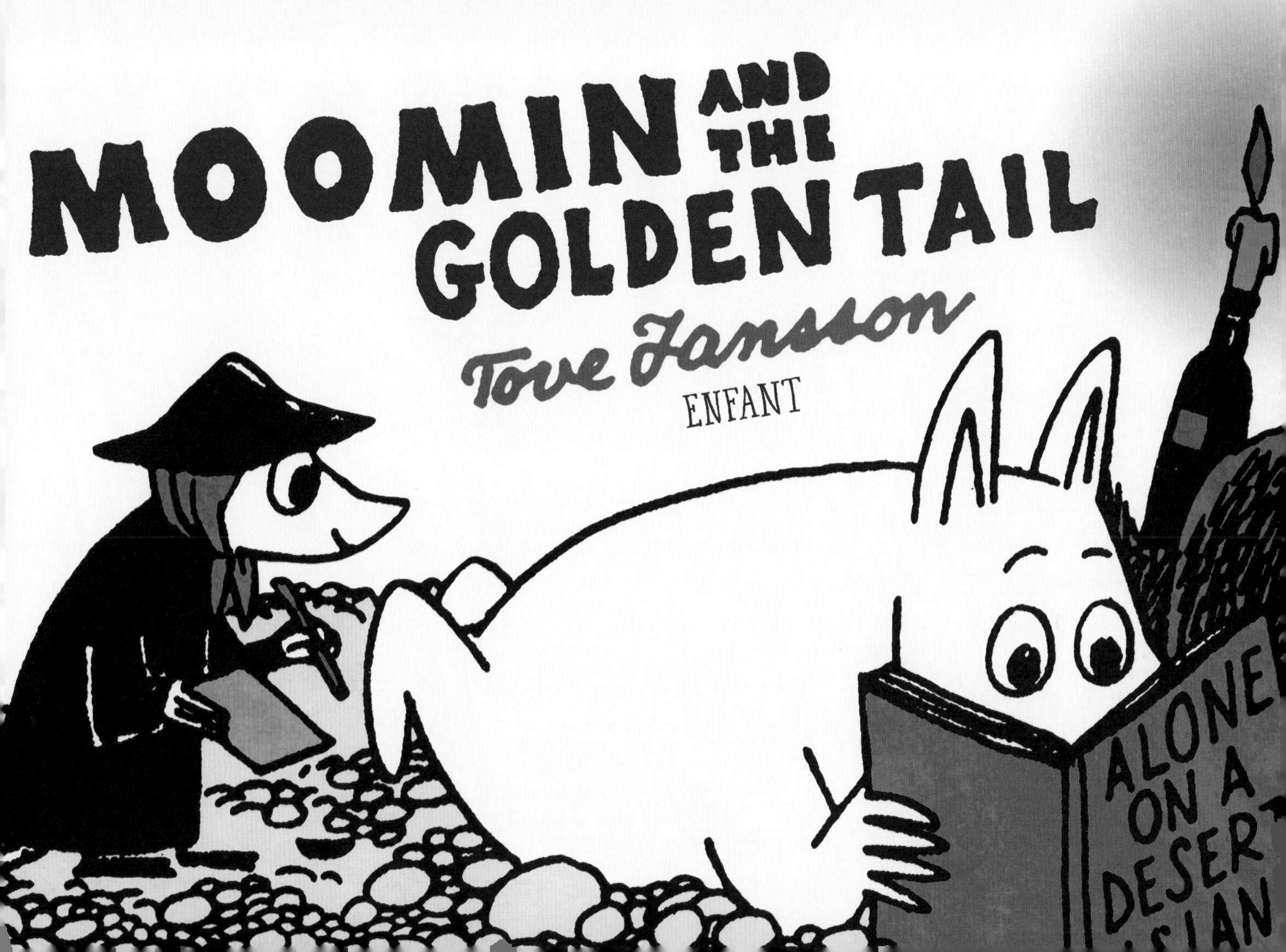
ALONE
ON A
DESERT

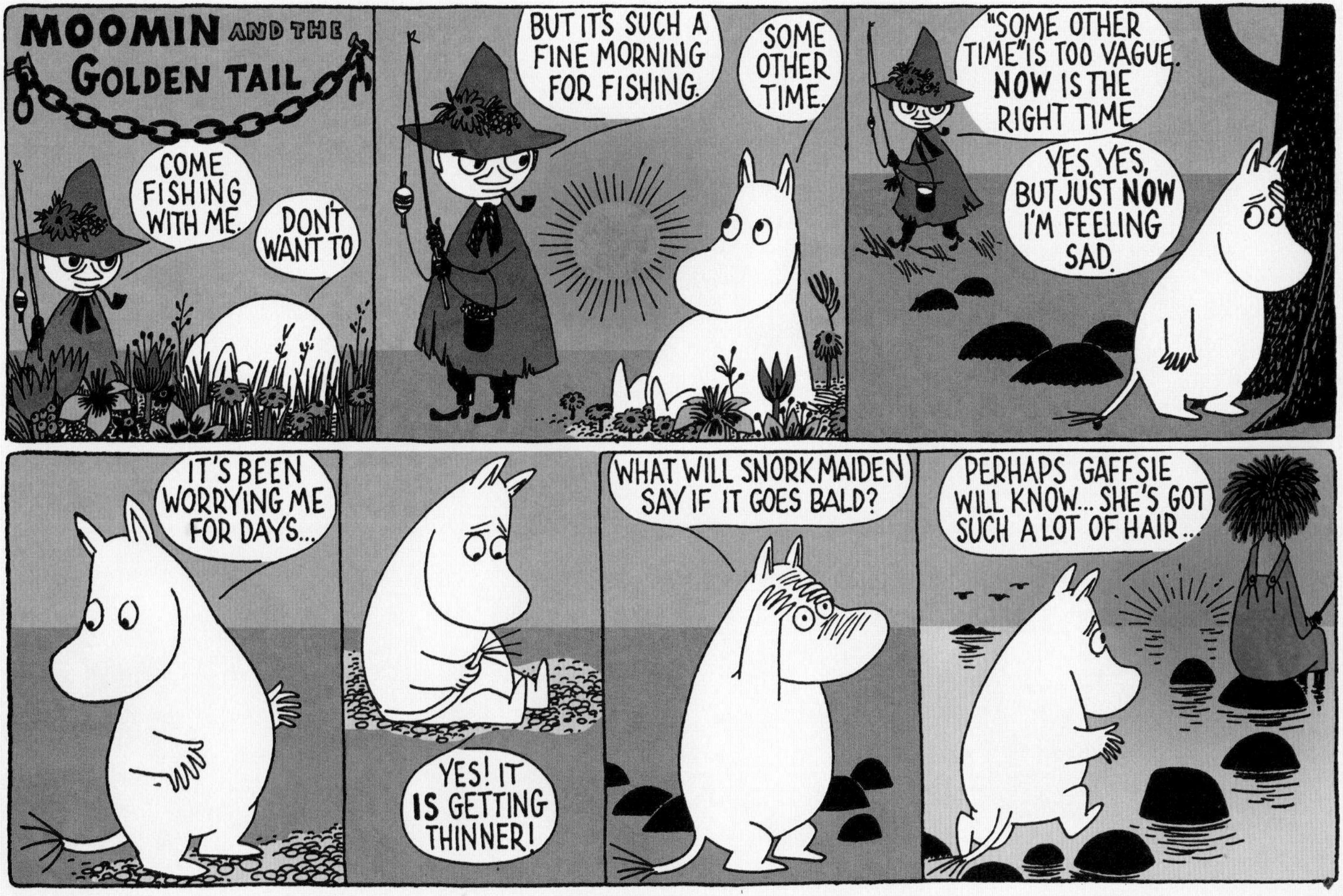
MOOMIN AND THE GOLDEN TAIL
COME FISHING WITH ME.
DON'T WANT TO
BUT IT'S SUCH A FINE MORNING FOR FISHING.
SOME OTHER TIME.
"SOME OTHER TIME" IS TOO VAGUE. NOW IS THE RIGHT TIME
YES, YES, BUT JUST NOW I'M FEELING SAD.
IT'S BEEN WORRYING ME FOR DAYS...
YES! IT IS GETTING THINNER!
WHAT WILL SNORKMAIDEN SAY IF IT GOES BALD?
PERHAPS GAFFSIE WILL KNOW... SHE'S GOT SUCH A LOT OF HAIR...

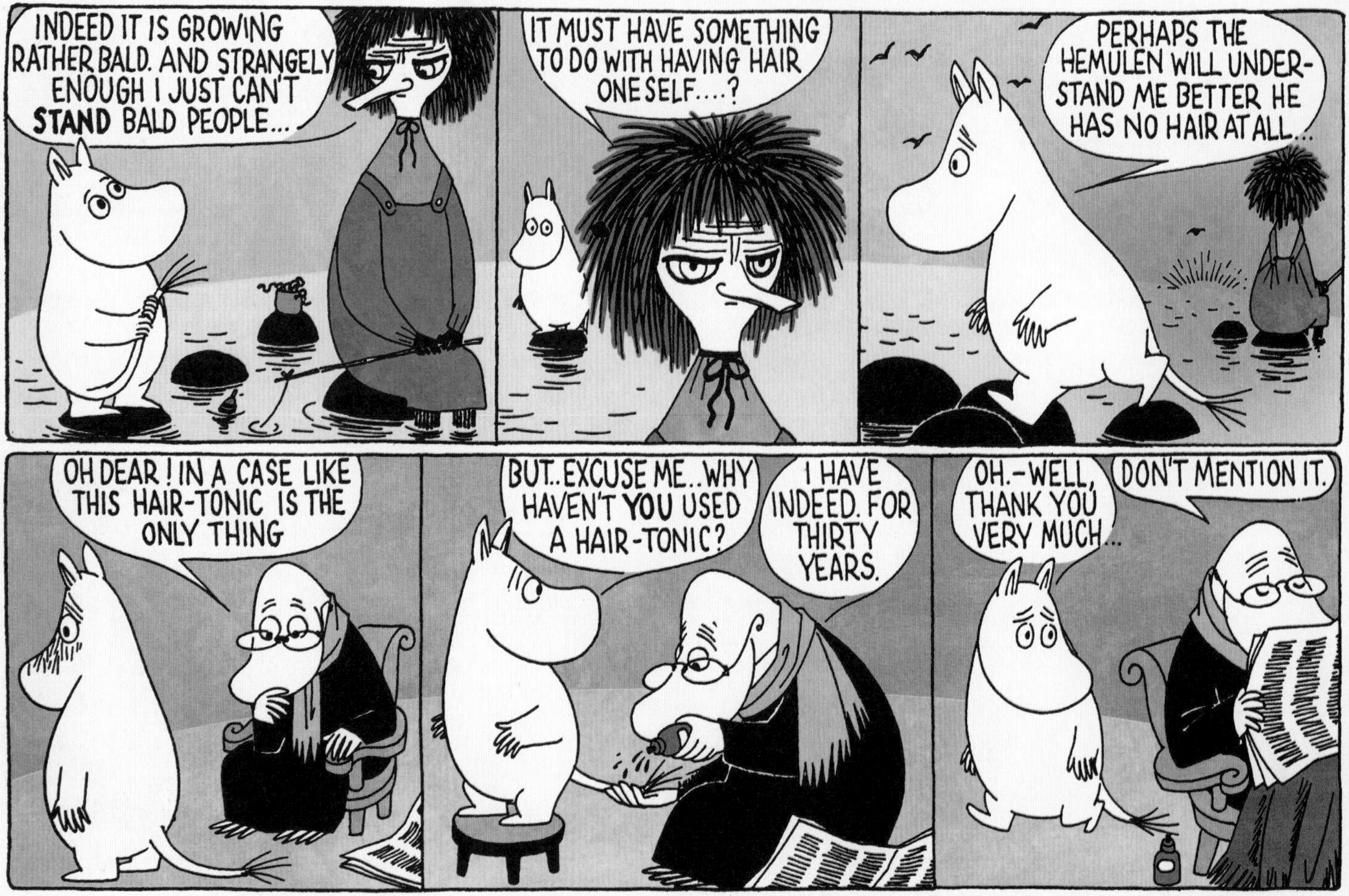
INDEED IT IS GROWING RATHER BALD. AND STRANGELY ENOUGH I JUST CAN'T STAND BALD PEOPLE...
IT MUST HAVE SOMETHING TO DO WITH HAVING HAIR ONESELF....?
PERHAPS THE HEMULEN WILL UNDERSTAND ME BETTER HE HAS NO HAIR AT ALL...
OH DEAR! IN A CASE LIKE THIS HAIR-TONIC IS THE ONLY THING
BUT..EXCUSE ME..WHY HAVEN'T YOU USED A HAIR-TONIC?
I HAVE INDEED. FOR THIRTY YEARS.
OH.-WELL, THANK YOU VERY MUCH...
DON'T MENTION IT.

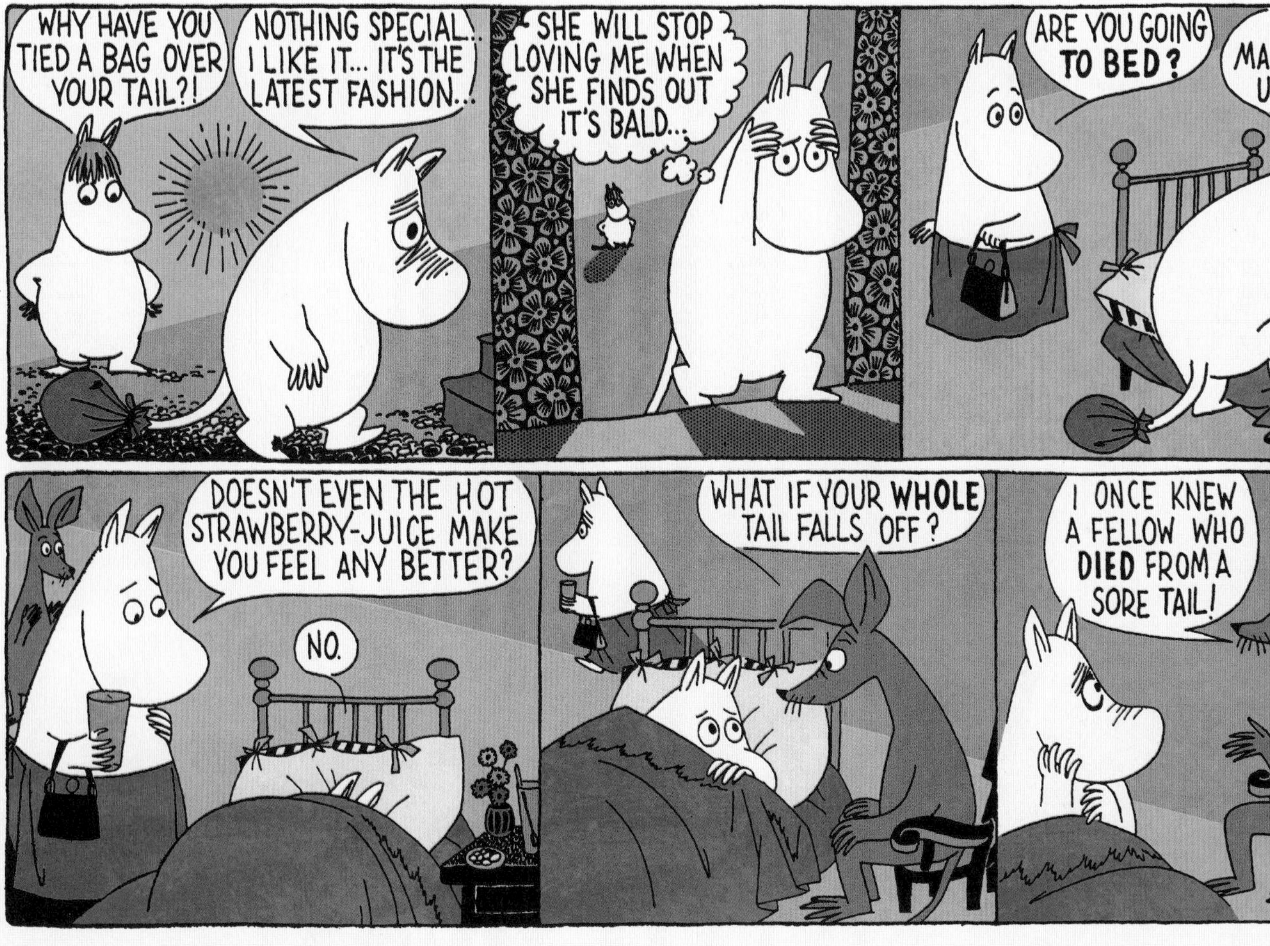
WHY HAVE YOU TIED A BAG OVER YOUR TAIL?!
NOTHING SPECIAL.. I LIKE IT... IT'S THE LATEST FASHION..!
SHE WILL STOP LOVING ME WHEN SHE FINDS OUT IT'S BALD...
ARE YOU GOING **TO BED?**
YES, MAMMA. I'M UNHAPPY.
DOESN'T EVEN THE HOT STRAWBERRY-JUICE MAKE YOU FEEL ANY BETTER?
NO.
WHAT IF YOUR **WHOLE** TAIL FALLS OFF?
I ONCE KNEW A FELLOW WHO **DIED** FROM A SORE TAIL!

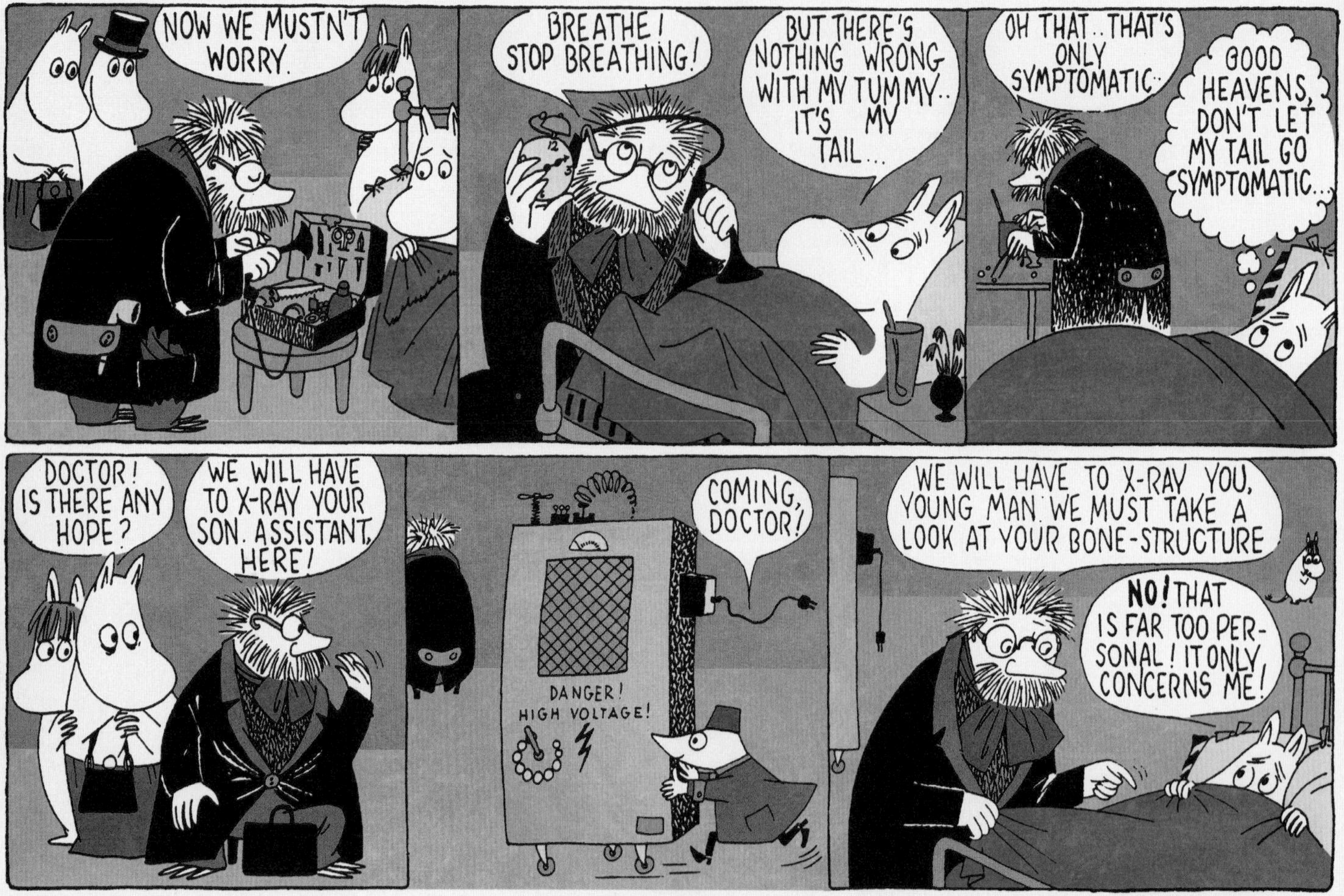
NOW WE MUSTN'T WORRY.
BREATHE! STOP BREATHING!
BUT THERE'S NOTHING WRONG WITH MY TUMMY.. IT'S MY TAIL...
OH THAT..THAT'S ONLY SYMPTOMATIC..
GOOD HEAVENS, DON'T LET MY TAIL GO SYMPTOMATIC...
DOCTOR! IS THERE ANY HOPE?
WE WILL HAVE TO X-RAY YOUR SON. ASSISTANT, HERE!
COMING, DOCTOR!
DANGER! HIGH VOLTAGE!
WE WILL HAVE TO X-RAY YOU, YOUNG MAN. WE MUST TAKE A LOOK AT YOUR BONE-STRUCTURE
NO! THAT IS FAR TOO PERSONAL! IT ONLY CONCERNS ME!

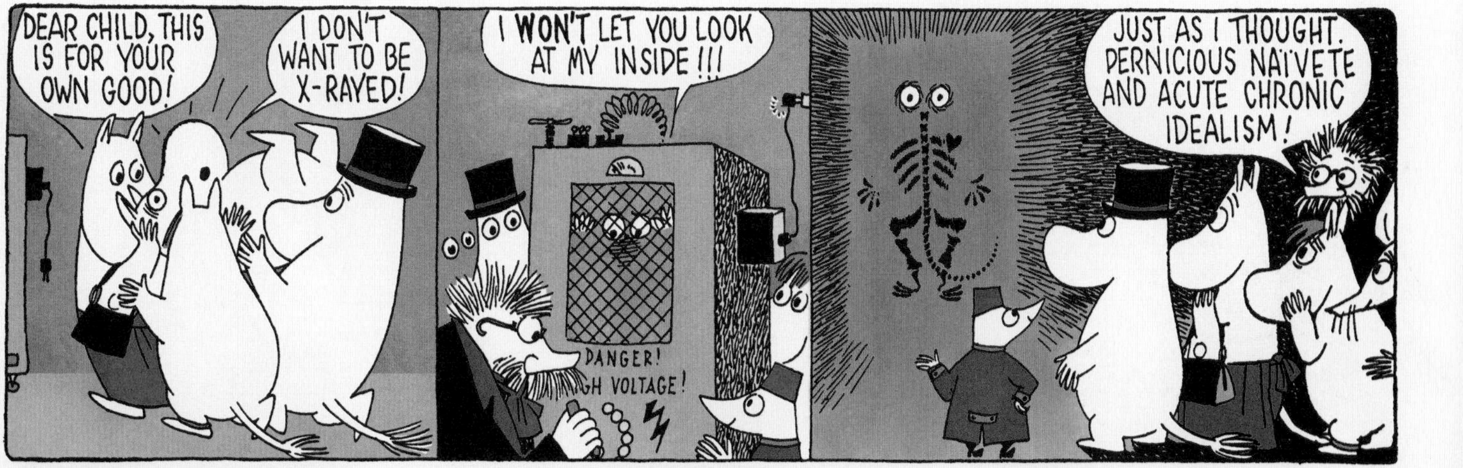
DEAR CHILD, THIS IS FOR YOUR OWN GOOD!
I DON'T WANT TO BE X-RAYED!
I WON'T LET YOU LOOK AT MY INSIDE!!!
DANGER! HIGH VOLTAGE!
JUST AS I THOUGHT. PERNICIOUS NAÏVETE AND ACUTE CHRONIC IDEALISM!

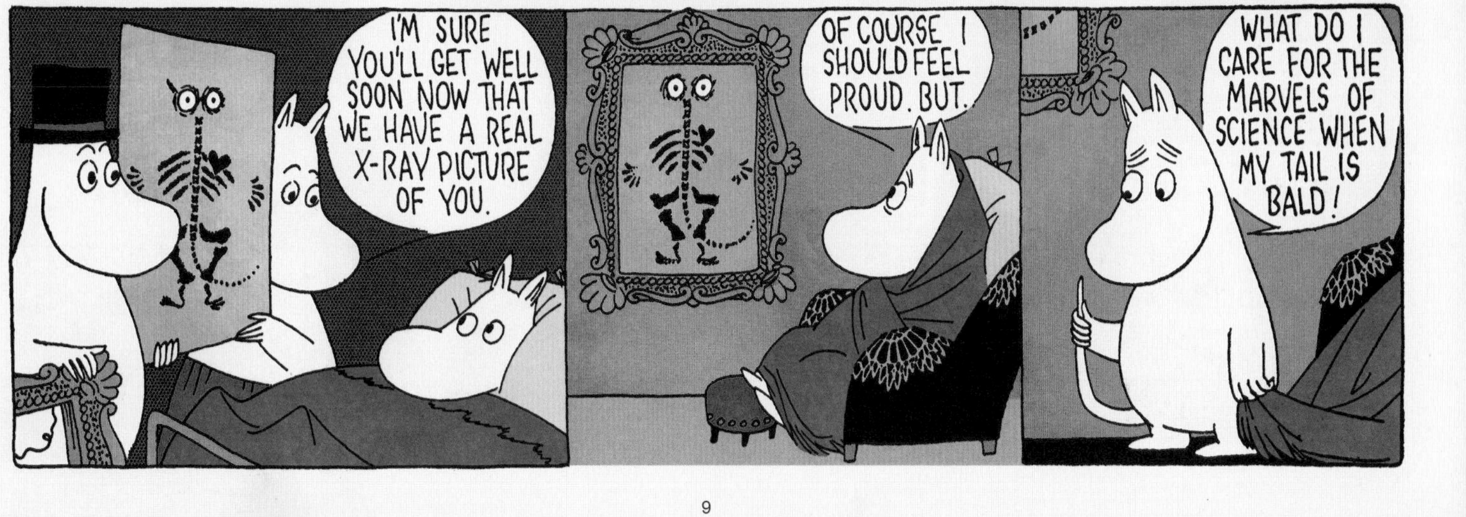
I'M SURE YOU'LL GET WELL SOON NOW THAT WE HAVE A REAL X-RAY PICTURE OF YOU.
OF COURSE I SHOULD FEEL PROUD. BUT...
WHAT DO I CARE FOR THE MARVELS OF SCIENCE WHEN MY TAIL IS BALD!

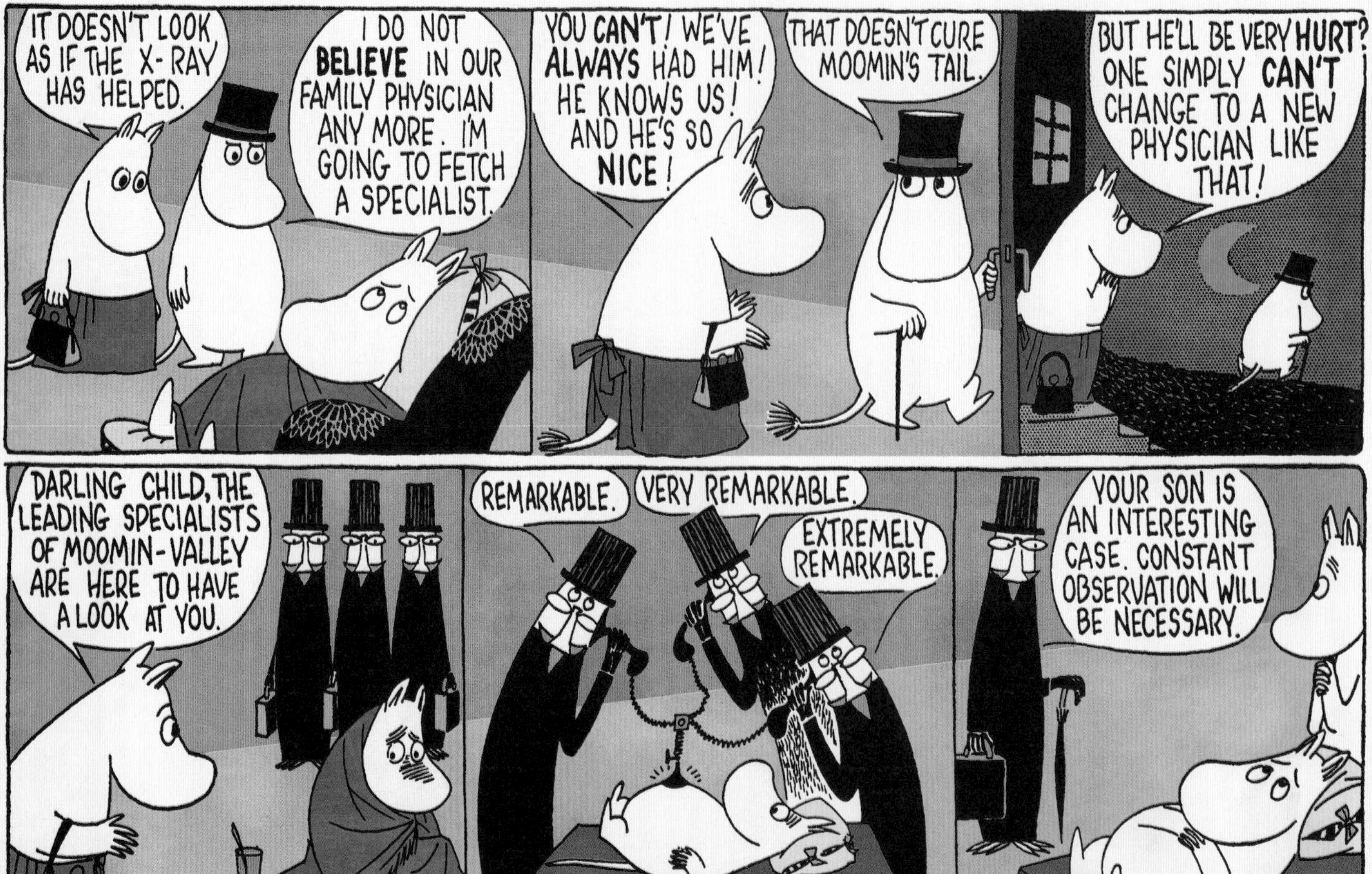
IT DOESN'T LOOK AS IF THE X-RAY HAS HELPED.
I DO NOT **BELIEVE** IN OUR FAMILY PHYSICIAN ANY MORE. I'M GOING TO FETCH A SPECIALIST.
YOU **CAN'T**! WE'VE **ALWAYS** HAD HIM! HE KNOWS US! AND HE'S SO **NICE**!
THAT DOESN'T CURE MOOMIN'S TAIL.
BUT HE'LL BE VERY **HURT**? ONE SIMPLY **CAN'T** CHANGE TO A NEW PHYSICIAN LIKE THAT!
DARLING CHILD, THE LEADING SPECIALISTS OF MOOMIN-VALLEY ARE HERE TO HAVE A LOOK AT YOU.
REMARKABLE.
VERY REMARKABLE.
EXTREMELY REMARKABLE.
YOUR SON IS AN INTERESTING CASE. CONSTANT OBSERVATION WILL BE NECESSARY.

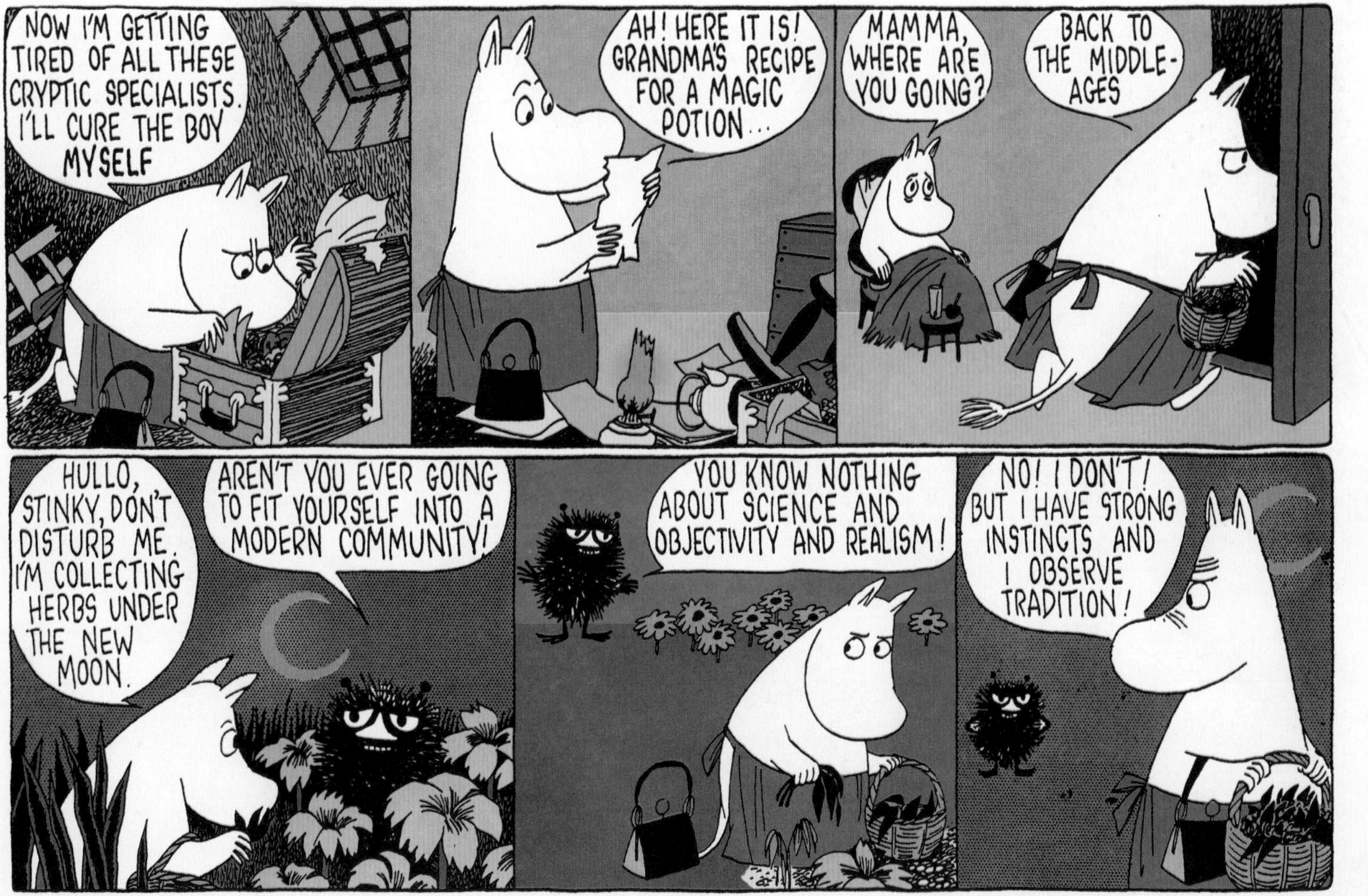
NOW I'M GETTING TIRED OF ALL THESE CRYPTIC SPECIALISTS. I'LL CURE THE BOY MYSELF
AH! HERE IT IS! GRANDMA'S RECIPE FOR A MAGIC POTION...
MAMMA, WHERE ARE YOU GOING?
BACK TO THE MIDDLE-AGES
HULLO, STINKY, DON'T DISTURB ME. I'M COLLECTING HERBS UNDER THE NEW MOON.
AREN'T YOU EVER GOING TO FIT YOURSELF INTO A MODERN COMMUNITY!
YOU KNOW NOTHING ABOUT SCIENCE AND OBJECTIVITY AND REALISM!
NO! I DON'T! BUT I HAVE STRONG INSTINCTS AND I OBSERVE TRADITION!

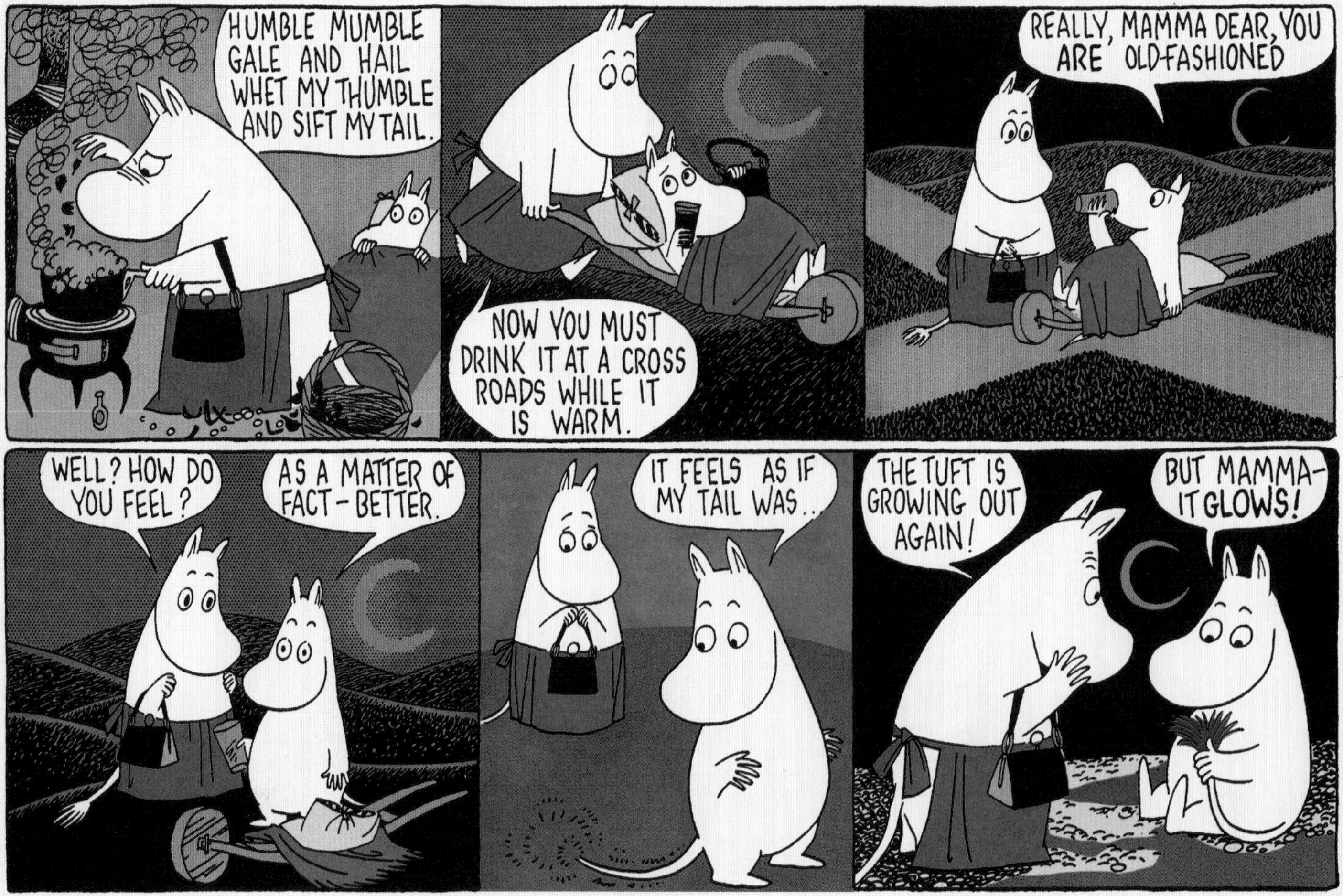
HUMBLE MUMBLE
GALE AND HAIL
WHET MY THUMBLE
AND SIFT MY TAIL.
NOW YOU MUST
DRINK IT AT A CROSS
ROADS WHILE IT
IS WARM.
REALLY, MAMMA DEAR, YOU
ARE OLD-FASHIONED
WELL? HOW DO
YOU FEEL?
AS A MATTER OF
FACT - BETTER.
IT FEELS AS IF
MY TAIL WAS...
THE TUFT IS
GROWING OUT
AGAIN!
BUT MAMMA-
IT GLOWS!

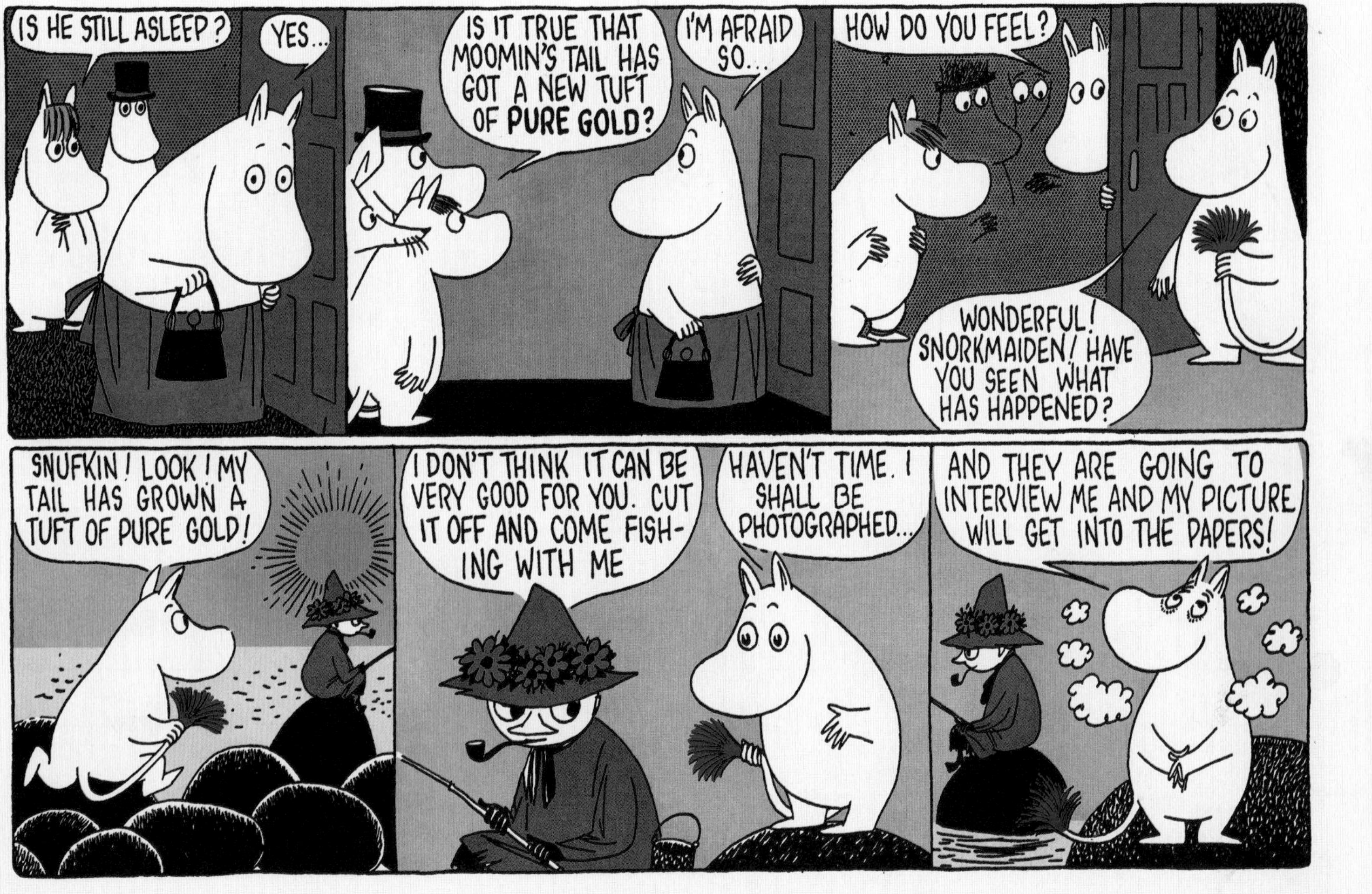
IS HE STILL ASLEEP?
YES...
IS IT TRUE THAT MOOMIN'S TAIL HAS GOT A NEW TUFT OF PURE GOLD?
I'M AFRAID SO...
HOW DO YOU FEEL?
WONDERFUL! SNORKMAIDEN! HAVE YOU SEEN WHAT HAS HAPPENED?
SNUFKIN! LOOK! MY TAIL HAS GROWN A TUFT OF PURE GOLD!
I DON'T THINK IT CAN BE VERY GOOD FOR YOU. CUT IT OFF AND COME FISHING WITH ME
HAVEN'T TIME. I SHALL BE PHOTOGRAPHED...
AND THEY ARE GOING TO INTERVIEW ME AND MY PICTURE WILL GET INTO THE PAPERS!

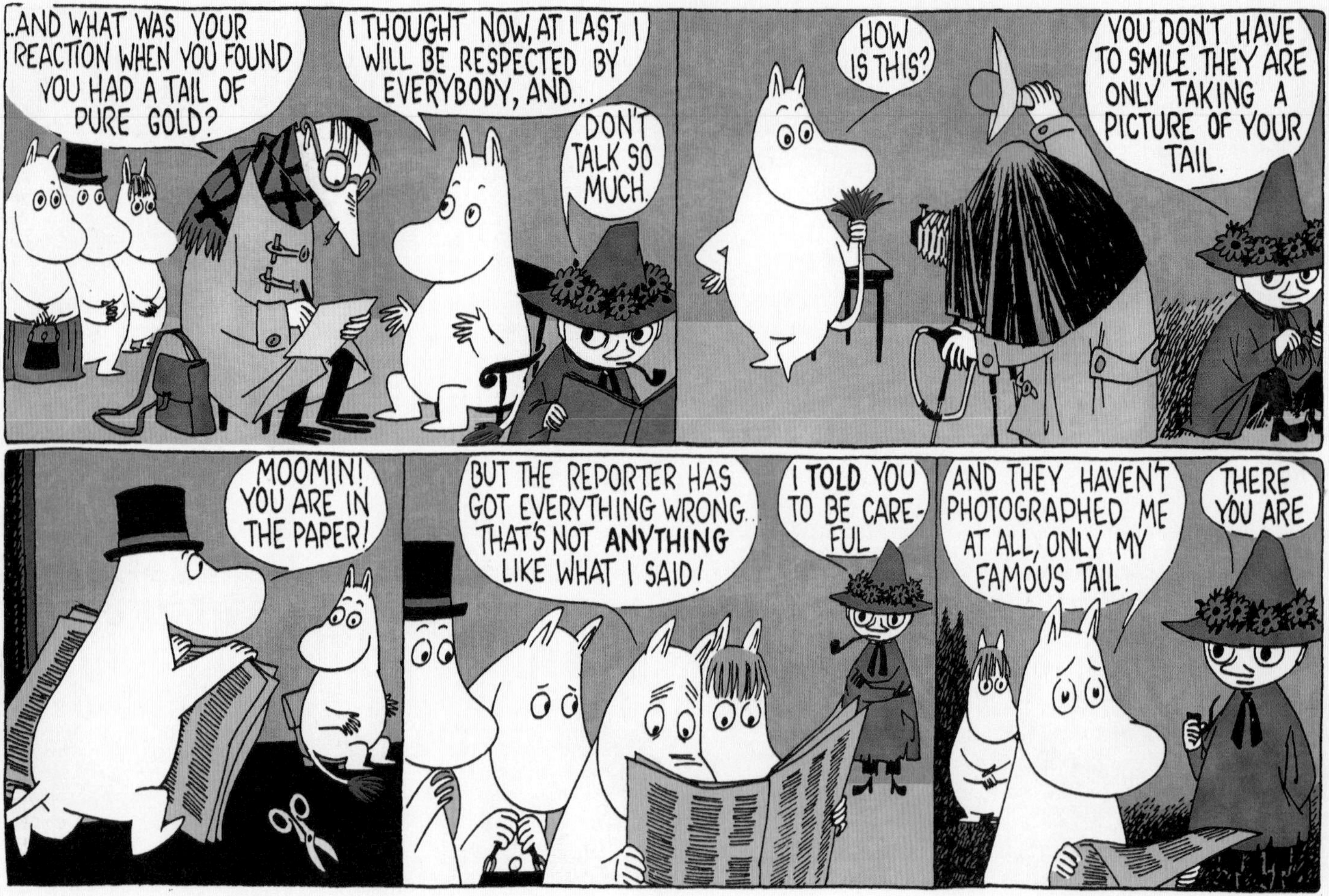
..AND WHAT WAS YOUR REACTION WHEN YOU FOUND YOU HAD A TAIL OF PURE GOLD?
I THOUGHT NOW, AT LAST, I WILL BE RESPECTED BY EVERYBODY, AND...
DON'T TALK SO MUCH.
HOW IS THIS?
YOU DON'T HAVE TO SMILE. THEY ARE ONLY TAKING A PICTURE OF YOUR TAIL.
MOOMIN! YOU ARE IN THE PAPER!
BUT THE REPORTER HAS GOT EVERYTHING WRONG... THAT'S NOT ANYTHING LIKE WHAT I SAID!
I TOLD YOU TO BE CARE-FUL
AND THEY HAVEN'T PHOTOGRAPHED ME AT ALL, ONLY MY FAMOUS TAIL.
THERE YOU ARE

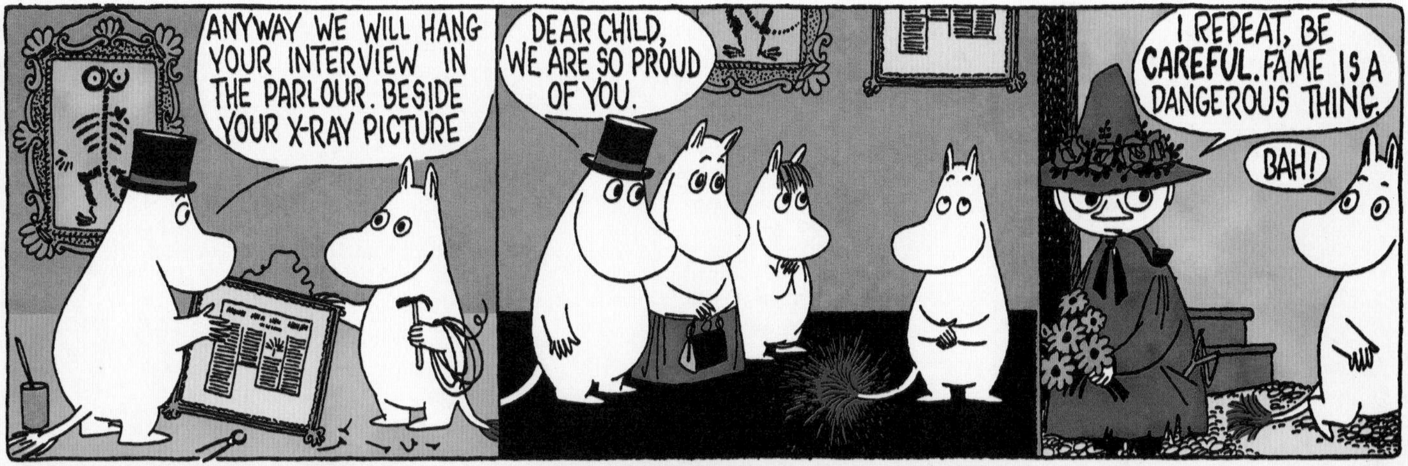
ANYWAY WE WILL HANG YOUR INTERVIEW IN THE PARLOUR. BESIDE YOUR X-RAY PICTURE
DEAR CHILD, WE ARE SO PROUD OF YOU.
I REPEAT, BE CAREFUL. FAME IS A DANGEROUS THING.
BAH!

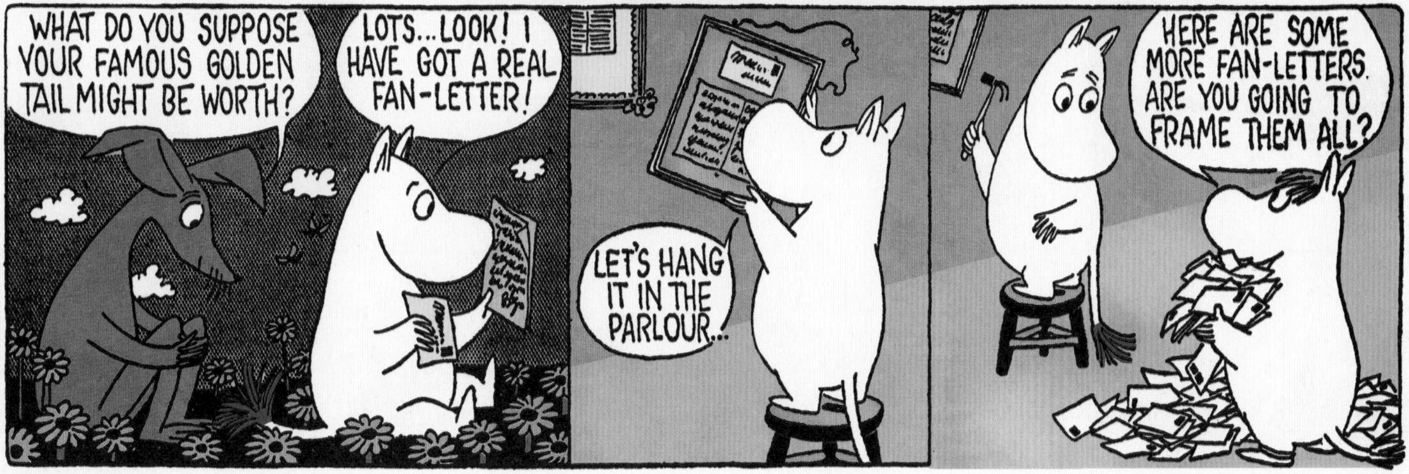
WHAT DO YOU SUPPOSE YOUR FAMOUS GOLDEN TAIL MIGHT BE WORTH?
LOTS...LOOK! I HAVE GOT A REAL FAN-LETTER!
LET'S HANG IT IN THE PARLOUR...
HERE ARE SOME MORE FAN-LETTERS. ARE YOU GOING TO FRAME THEM ALL?

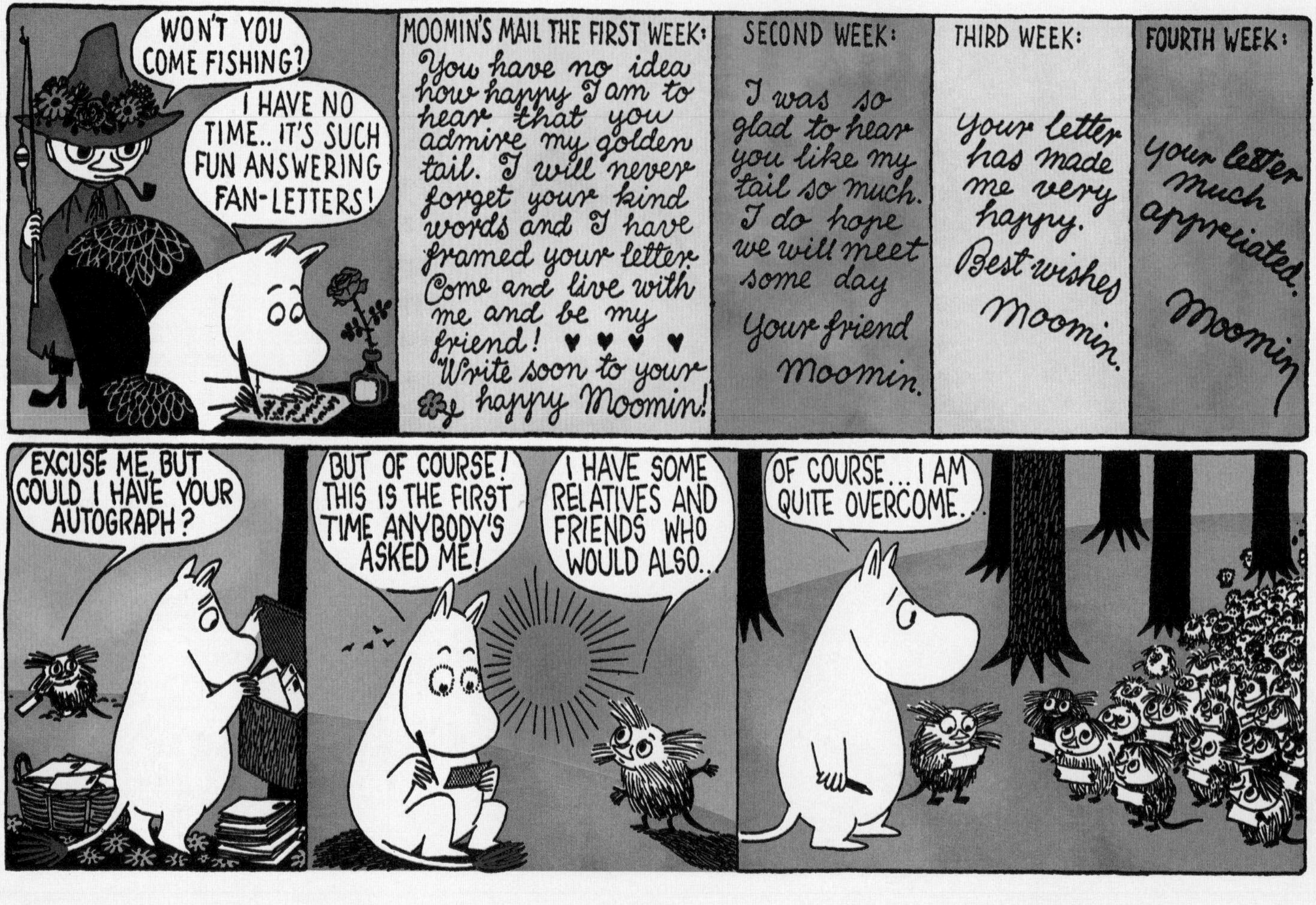

WON'T YOU COME FISHING?
I HAVE NO TIME.. IT'S SUCH FUN ANSWERING FAN-LETTERS!
MOOMIN'S MAIL THE FIRST WEEK:
You have no idea how happy I am to hear that you admire my golden tail. I will never forget your kind words and I have framed your letter. Come and live with me and be my friend! ♥ ♥ ♥ ♥
Write soon to your happy Moomin!
SECOND WEEK:
I was so glad to hear you like my tail so much. I do hope we will meet some day
Your friend Moomin.
THIRD WEEK:
Your letter has made me very happy.
Best wishes Moomin.
FOURTH WEEK:
Your letter much appreciated.
Moomin
EXCUSE ME, BUT COULD I HAVE YOUR AUTOGRAPH?
BUT OF COURSE! THIS IS THE FIRST TIME ANYBODY'S ASKED ME!
I HAVE SOME RELATIVES AND FRIENDS WHO WOULD ALSO...
OF COURSE... I AM QUITE OVERCOME...

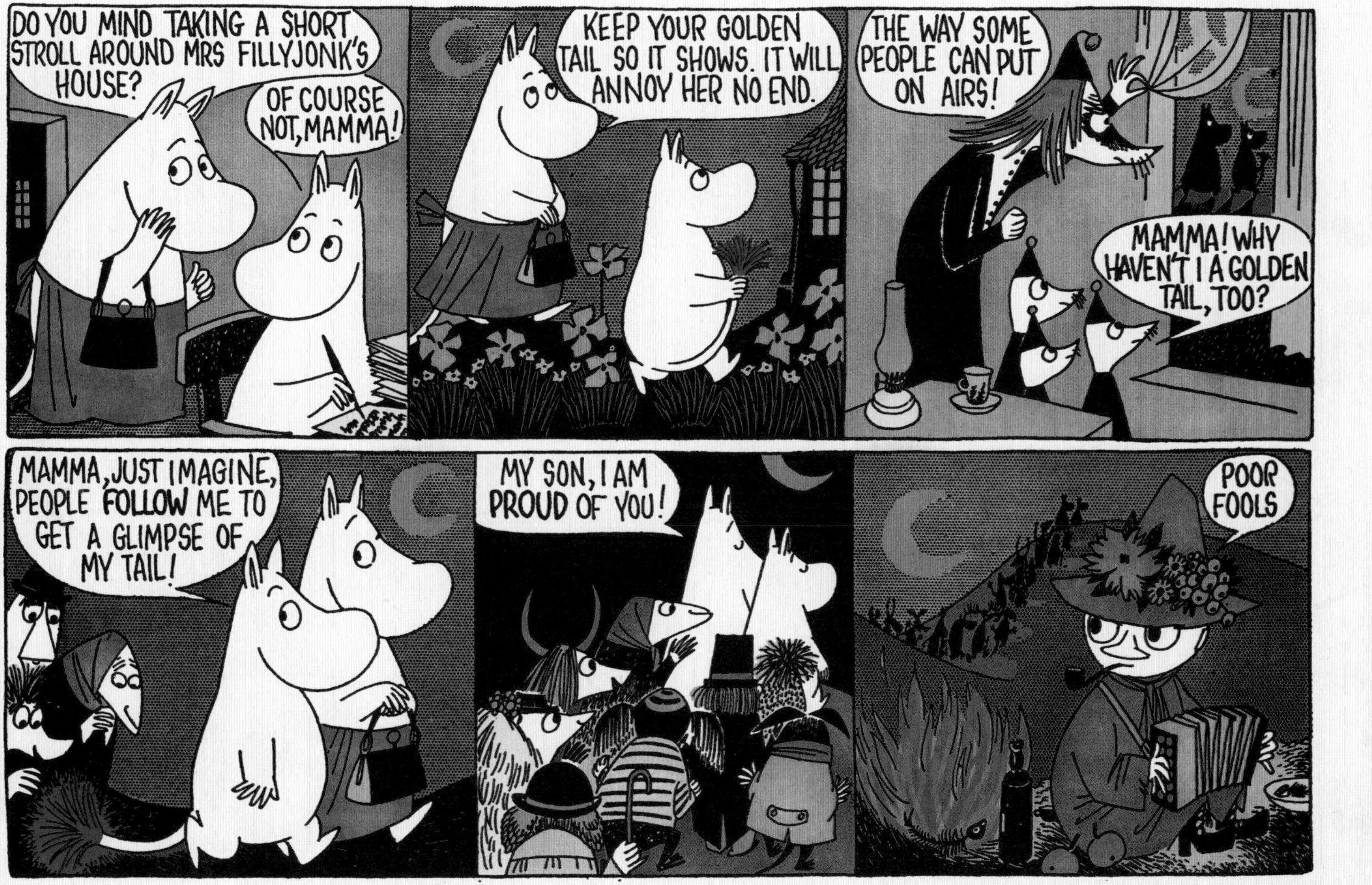
DO YOU MIND TAKING A SHORT STROLL AROUND MRS FILLYJONK'S HOUSE?
OF COURSE NOT, MAMMA!
KEEP YOUR GOLDEN TAIL SO IT SHOWS. IT WILL ANNOY HER NO END.
THE WAY SOME PEOPLE CAN PUT ON AIRS!
MAMMA! WHY HAVEN'T I A GOLDEN TAIL, TOO?
MAMMA, JUST IMAGINE, PEOPLE FOLLOW ME TO GET A GLIMPSE OF MY TAIL!
MY SON, I AM PROUD OF YOU!
POOR FOOLS

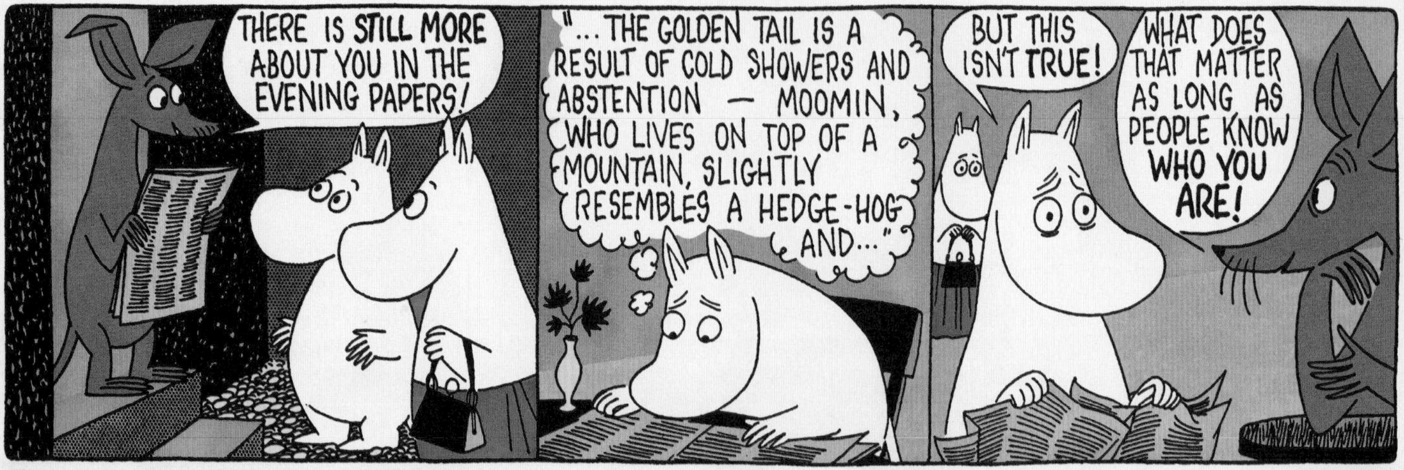
THERE IS STILL MORE ABOUT YOU IN THE EVENING PAPERS!
"... THE GOLDEN TAIL IS A RESULT OF COLD SHOWERS AND ABSTENTION — MOOMIN, WHO LIVES ON TOP OF A MOUNTAIN, SLIGHTLY RESEMBLES A HEDGE-HOG AND..."
BUT THIS ISN'T TRUE!
WHAT DOES THAT MATTER AS LONG AS PEOPLE KNOW WHO YOU ARE!

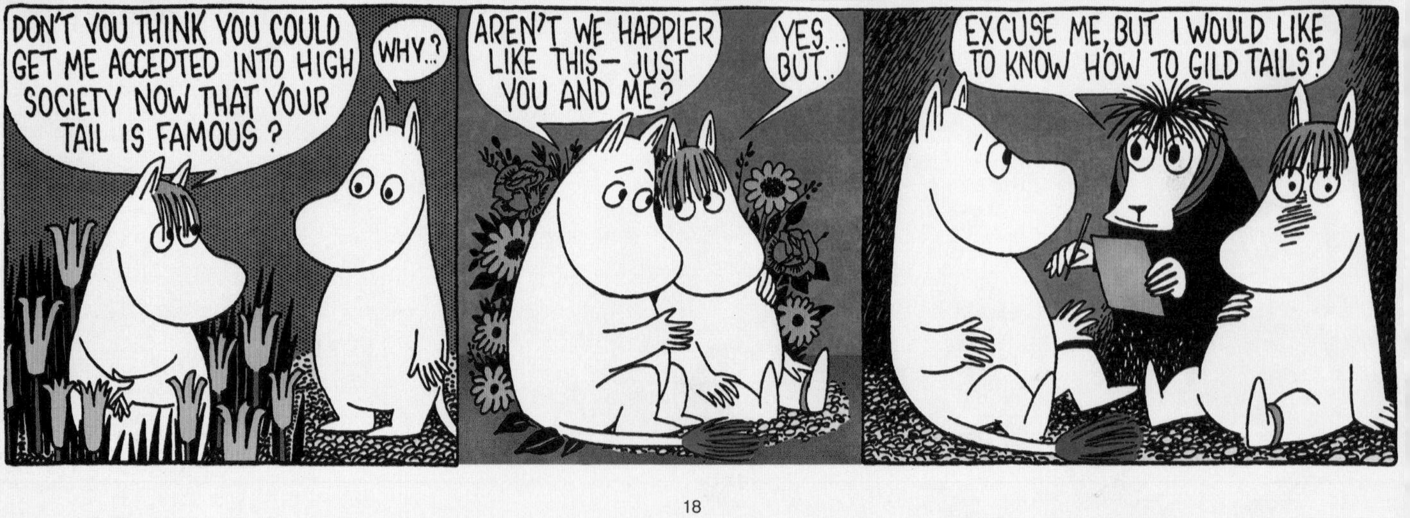
DON'T YOU THINK YOU COULD GET ME ACCEPTED INTO HIGH SOCIETY NOW THAT YOUR TAIL IS FAMOUS ?
WHY..?
AREN'T WE HAPPIER LIKE THIS— JUST YOU AND ME?
YES... BUT..
EXCUSE ME, BUT I WOULD LIKE TO KNOW HOW TO GILD TAILS?

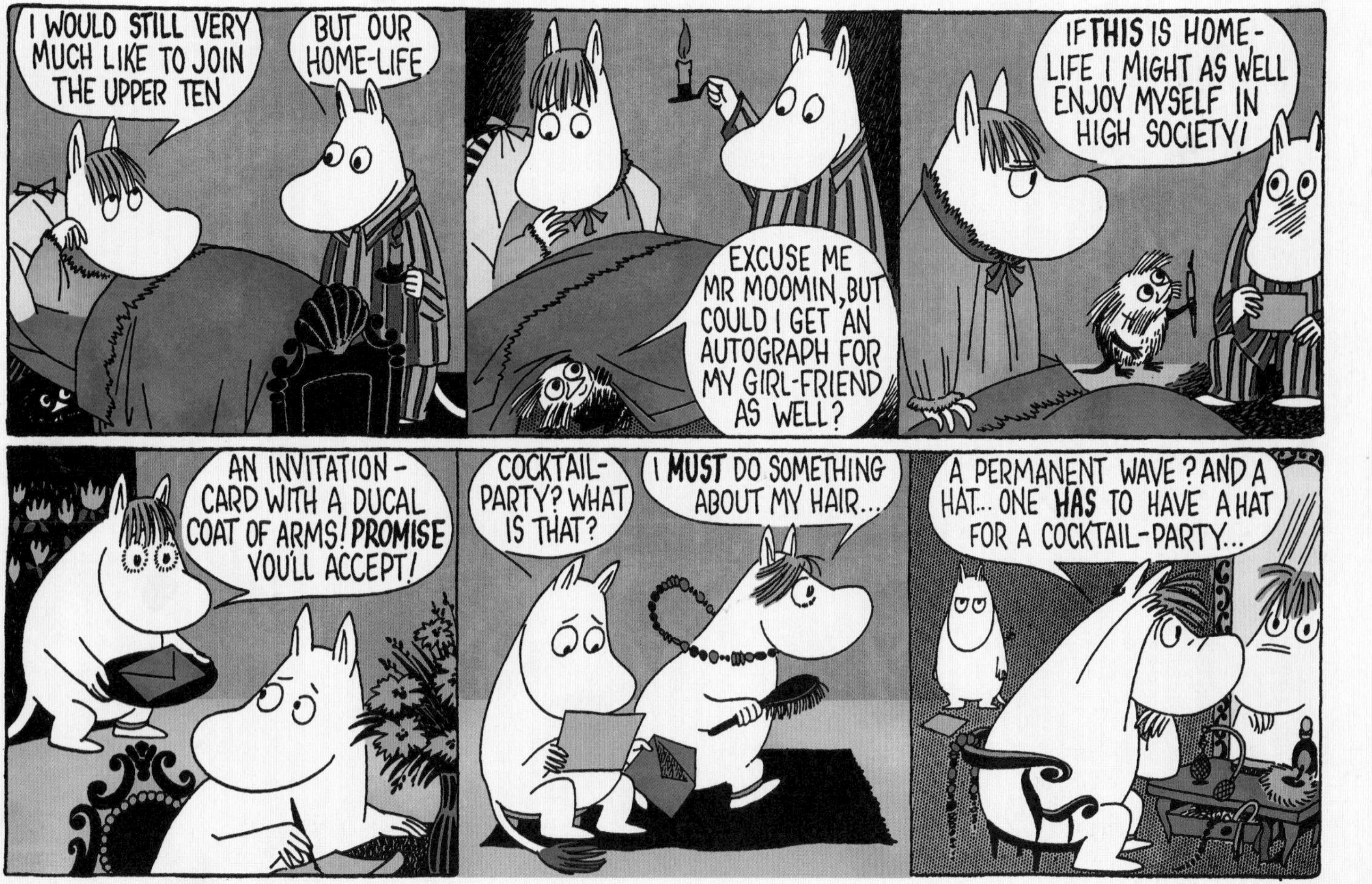
I WOULD STILL VERY MUCH LIKE TO JOIN THE UPPER TEN
BUT OUR HOME-LIFE
EXCUSE ME MR MOOMIN, BUT COULD I GET AN AUTOGRAPH FOR MY GIRL-FRIEND AS WELL?
IF THIS IS HOME-LIFE I MIGHT AS WELL ENJOY MYSELF IN HIGH SOCIETY!
AN INVITATION-CARD WITH A DUCAL COAT OF ARMS! PROMISE YOU'LL ACCEPT!
COCKTAIL-PARTY? WHAT IS THAT?
I MUST DO SOMETHING ABOUT MY HAIR...
A PERMANENT WAVE? AND A HAT... ONE HAS TO HAVE A HAT FOR A COCKTAIL-PARTY...

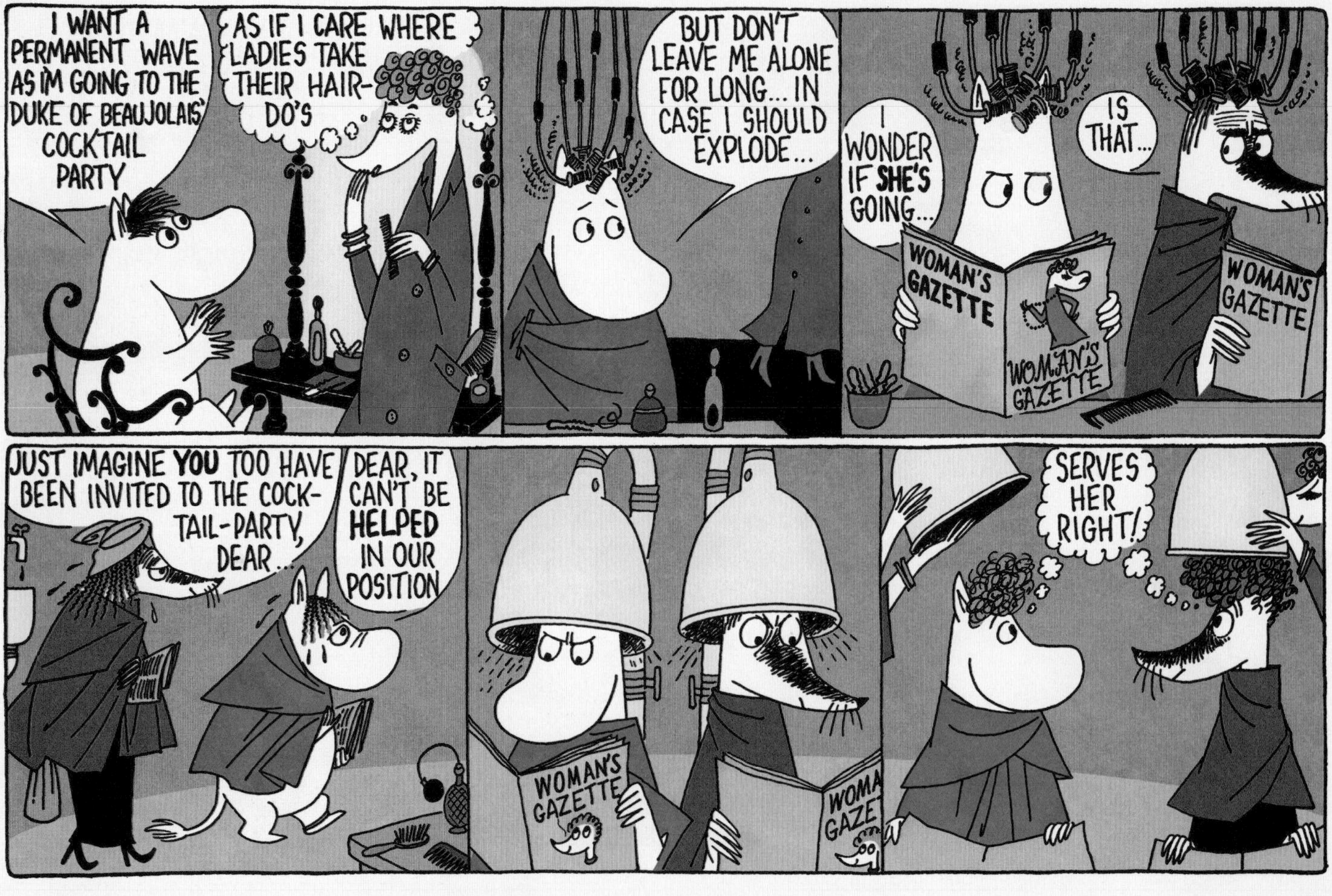
I WANT A PERMANENT WAVE AS I'M GOING TO THE DUKE OF BEAUJOLAIS' COCKTAIL PARTY
AS IF I CARE WHERE LADIES TAKE THEIR HAIR-DO'S
BUT DON'T LEAVE ME ALONE FOR LONG... IN CASE I SHOULD EXPLODE...
I WONDER IF SHE'S GOING...
IS THAT...
WOMAN'S GAZETTE
WOMAN'S GAZETTE
WOMAN'S GAZETTE
JUST IMAGINE YOU TOO HAVE BEEN INVITED TO THE COCK-TAIL-PARTY, DEAR...
DEAR, IT CAN'T BE HELPED IN OUR POSITION
WOMAN'S GAZETTE
SERVES HER RIGHT!

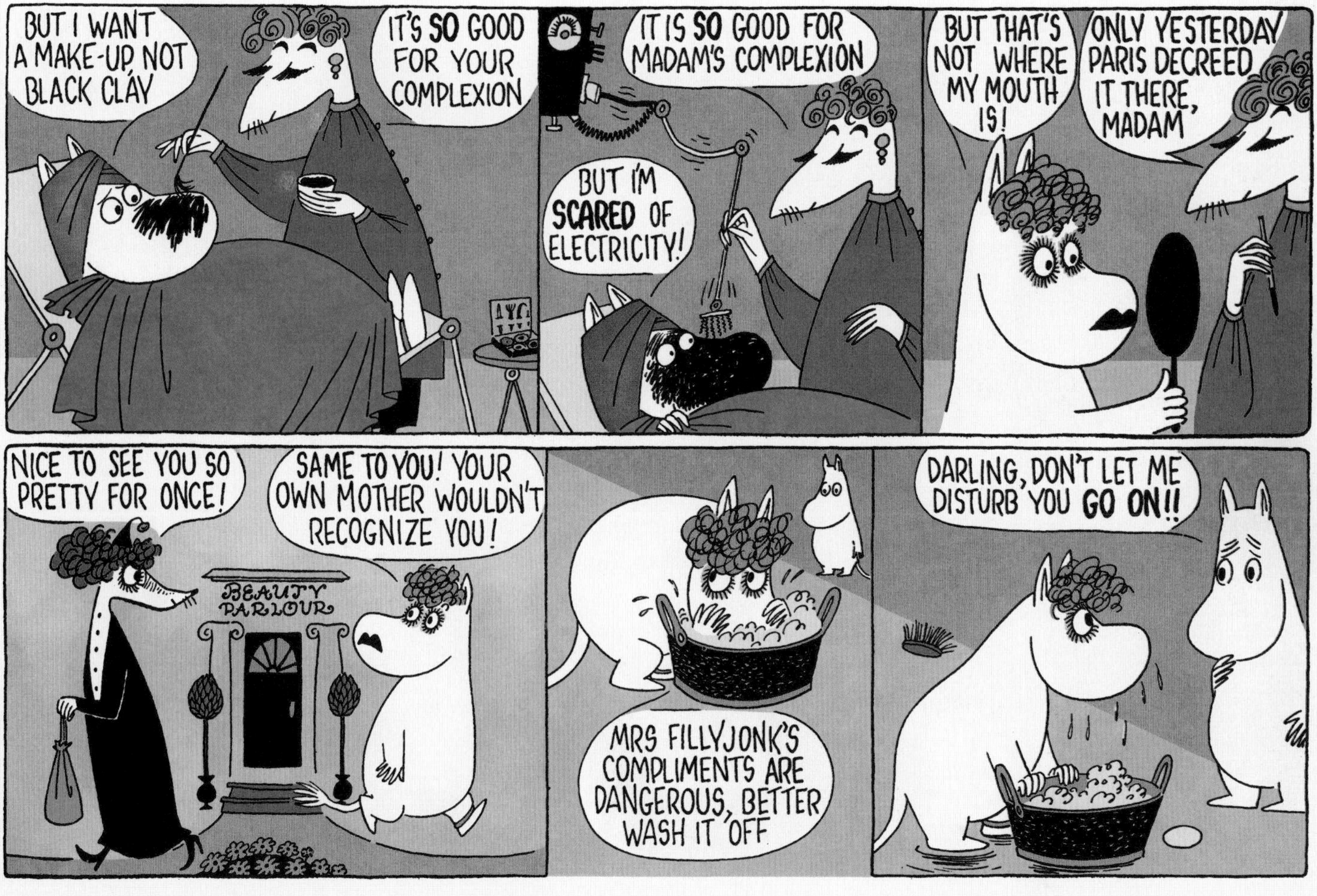

BUT I WANT A MAKE-UP NOT BLACK CLAY
IT'S SO GOOD FOR YOUR COMPLEXION
IT IS SO GOOD FOR MADAM'S COMPLEXION
BUT I'M SCARED OF ELECTRICITY!
BUT THAT'S NOT WHERE MY MOUTH IS!
ONLY YESTERDAY PARIS DECREED IT THERE, MADAM
NICE TO SEE YOU SO PRETTY FOR ONCE!
SAME TO YOU! YOUR OWN MOTHER WOULDN'T RECOGNIZE YOU!
BEAUTY PARLOUR
MRS FILLYJONK'S COMPLIMENTS ARE DANGEROUS, BETTER WASH IT OFF
DARLING, DON'T LET ME DISTURB YOU GO ON!!

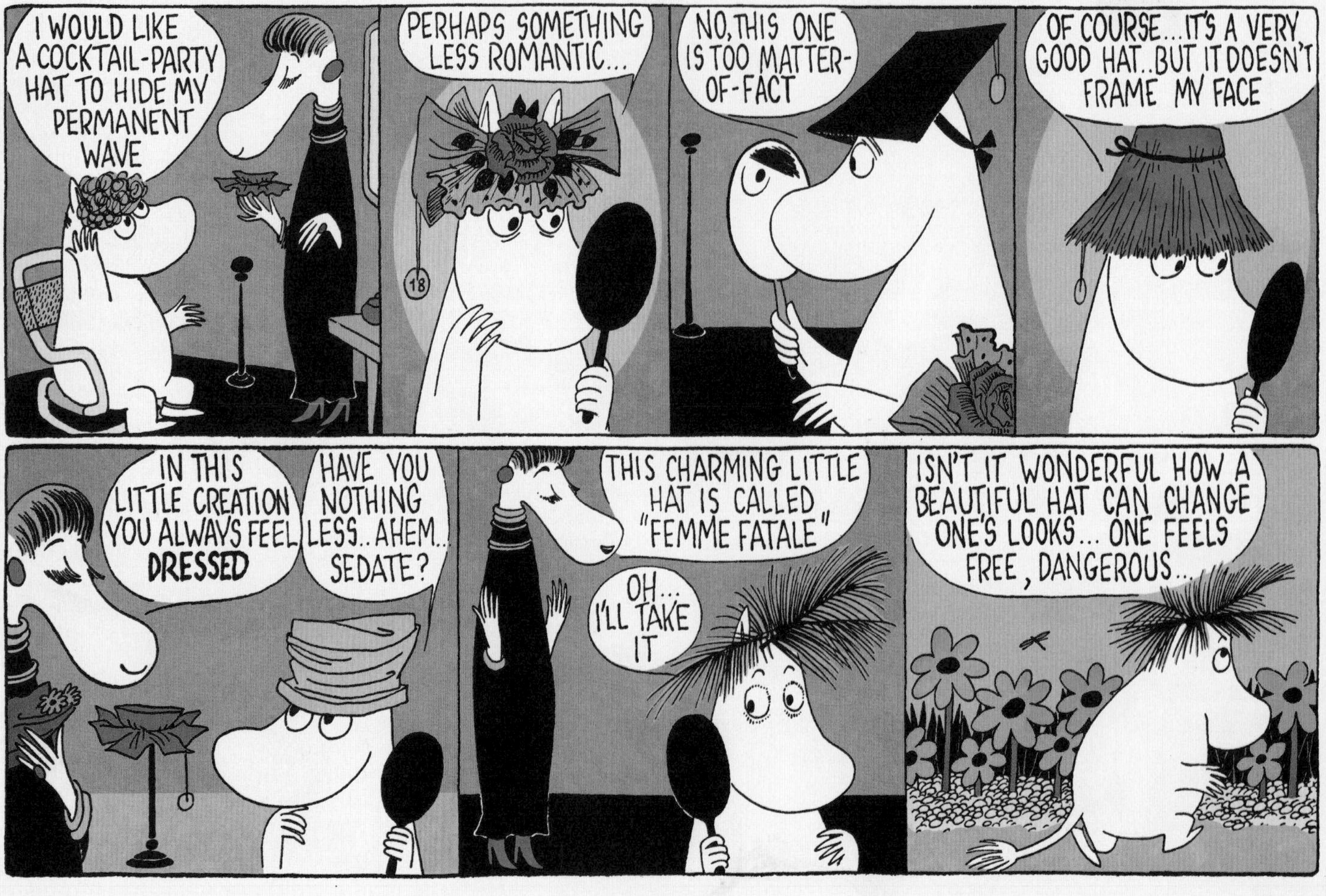
I WOULD LIKE A COCKTAIL-PARTY HAT TO HIDE MY PERMANENT WAVE
PERHAPS SOMETHING LESS ROMANTIC...
18
NO, THIS ONE IS TOO MATTER-OF-FACT
OF COURSE... IT'S A VERY GOOD HAT.. BUT IT DOESN'T FRAME MY FACE
IN THIS LITTLE CREATION YOU ALWAYS FEEL **DRESSED**
HAVE YOU NOTHING LESS.. AHEM.. SEDATE?
THIS CHARMING LITTLE HAT IS CALLED "FEMME FATALE"
OH... I'LL TAKE IT
ISN'T IT WONDERFUL HOW A BEAUTIFUL HAT CAN CHANGE ONE'S LOOKS... ONE FEELS FREE, DANGEROUS...

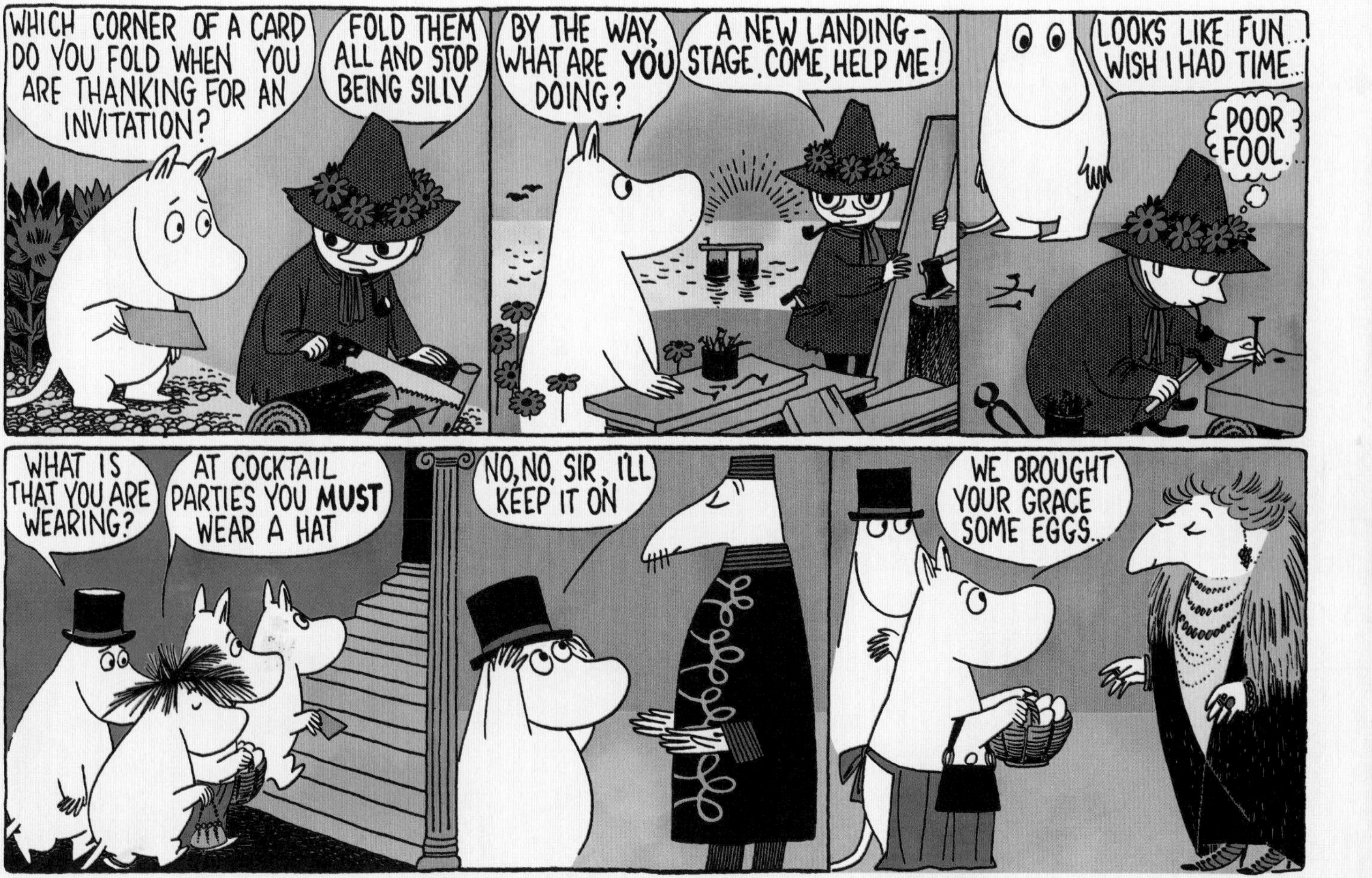
WHICH CORNER OF A CARD DO YOU FOLD WHEN YOU ARE THANKING FOR AN INVITATION?
FOLD THEM ALL AND STOP BEING SILLY
BY THE WAY, WHAT ARE **YOU** DOING?
A NEW LANDING-STAGE. COME, HELP ME!
LOOKS LIKE FUN... WISH I HAD TIME...
POOR FOOL...
WHAT IS THAT YOU ARE WEARING?
AT COCKTAIL PARTIES YOU **MUST** WEAR A HAT
NO, NO, SIR, I'LL KEEP IT ON
WE BROUGHT YOUR GRACE SOME EGGS...

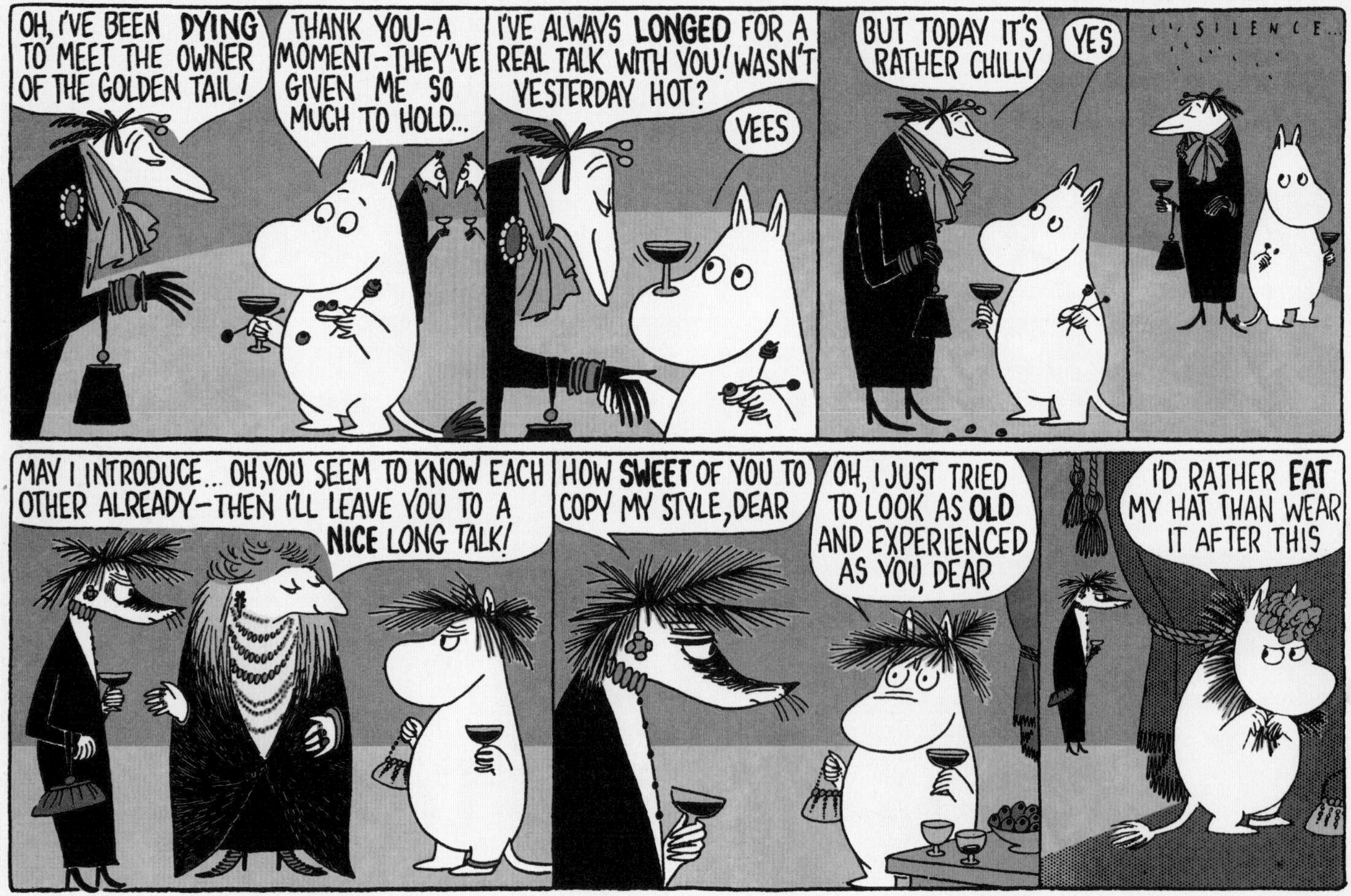

OH, I'VE BEEN **DYING** TO MEET THE OWNER OF THE GOLDEN TAIL!
THANK YOU–A MOMENT–THEY'VE GIVEN ME SO MUCH TO HOLD...
I'VE ALWAYS **LONGED** FOR A REAL TALK WITH YOU! WASN'T YESTERDAY HOT?
YEES
BUT TODAY IT'S RATHER CHILLY
YES
S I L E N C E...
MAY I INTRODUCE... OH,YOU SEEM TO KNOW EACH OTHER ALREADY–THEN I'LL LEAVE YOU TO A **NICE** LONG TALK!
HOW **SWEET** OF YOU TO COPY MY STYLE, DEAR
OH, I JUST TRIED TO LOOK AS **OLD** AND EXPERIENCED AS YOU, DEAR
I'D RATHER **EAT** MY HAT THAN WEAR IT AFTER THIS

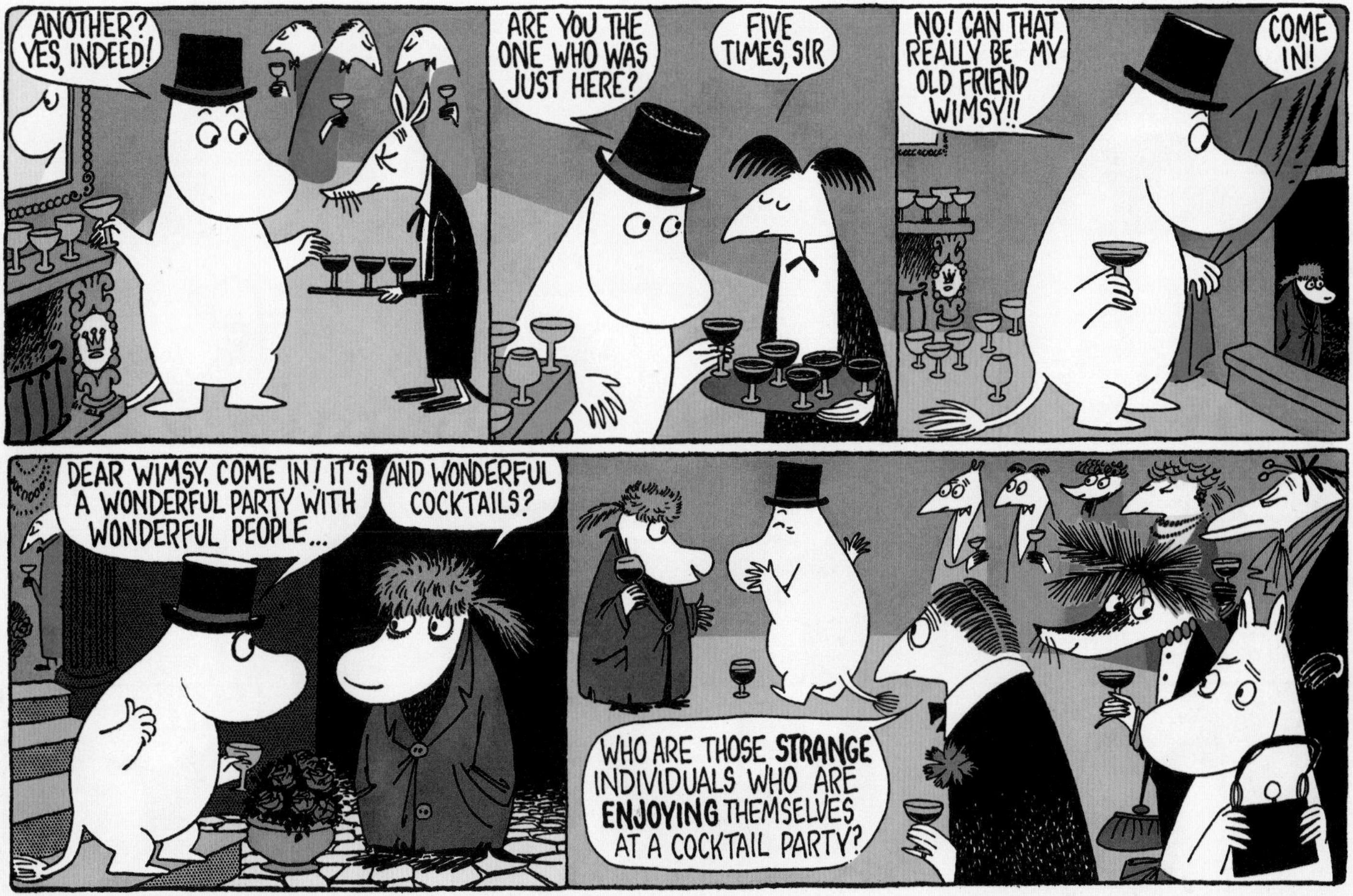
ANOTHER? YES, INDEED!
ARE YOU THE ONE WHO WAS JUST HERE?
FIVE TIMES, SIR
NO! CAN THAT REALLY BE MY OLD FRIEND WIMSY!!
COME IN!
DEAR WIMSY, COME IN! IT'S A WONDERFUL PARTY WITH WONDERFUL PEOPLE...
AND WONDERFUL COCKTAILS?
WHO ARE THOSE STRANGE INDIVIDUALS WHO ARE ENJOYING THEMSELVES AT A COCKTAIL PARTY?

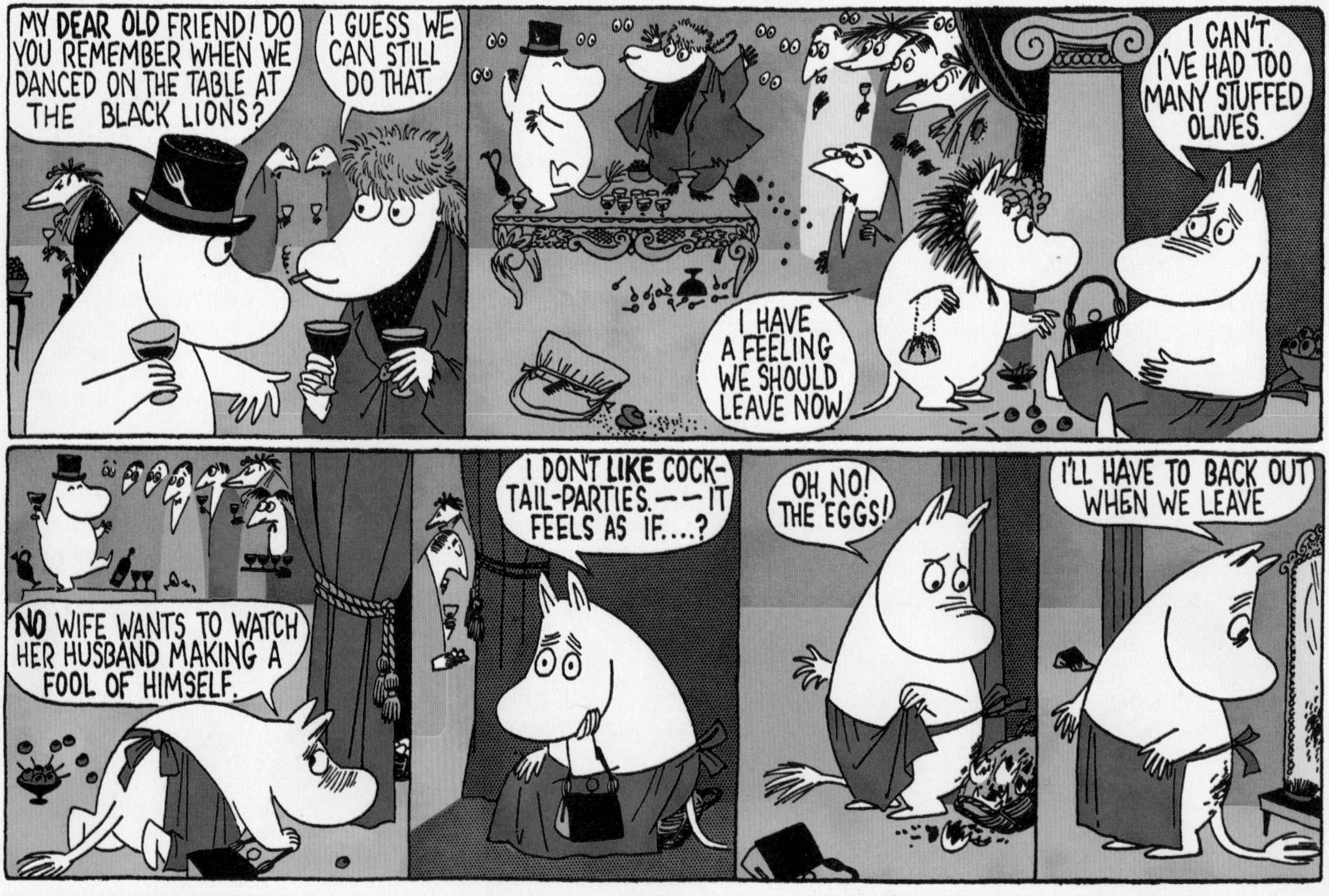
MY **DEAR OLD** FRIEND! DO YOU REMEMBER WHEN WE DANCED ON THE TABLE AT THE BLACK LIONS?
I GUESS WE CAN STILL DO THAT.
I CAN'T. I'VE HAD TOO MANY STUFFED OLIVES.
I HAVE A FEELING WE SHOULD LEAVE NOW
NO WIFE WANTS TO WATCH HER HUSBAND MAKING A FOOL OF HIMSELF.
I DON'T **LIKE** COCK-TAIL-PARTIES.—— IT FEELS AS IF....?
OH, NO! THE EGGS!
I'LL HAVE TO BACK OUT WHEN WE LEAVE

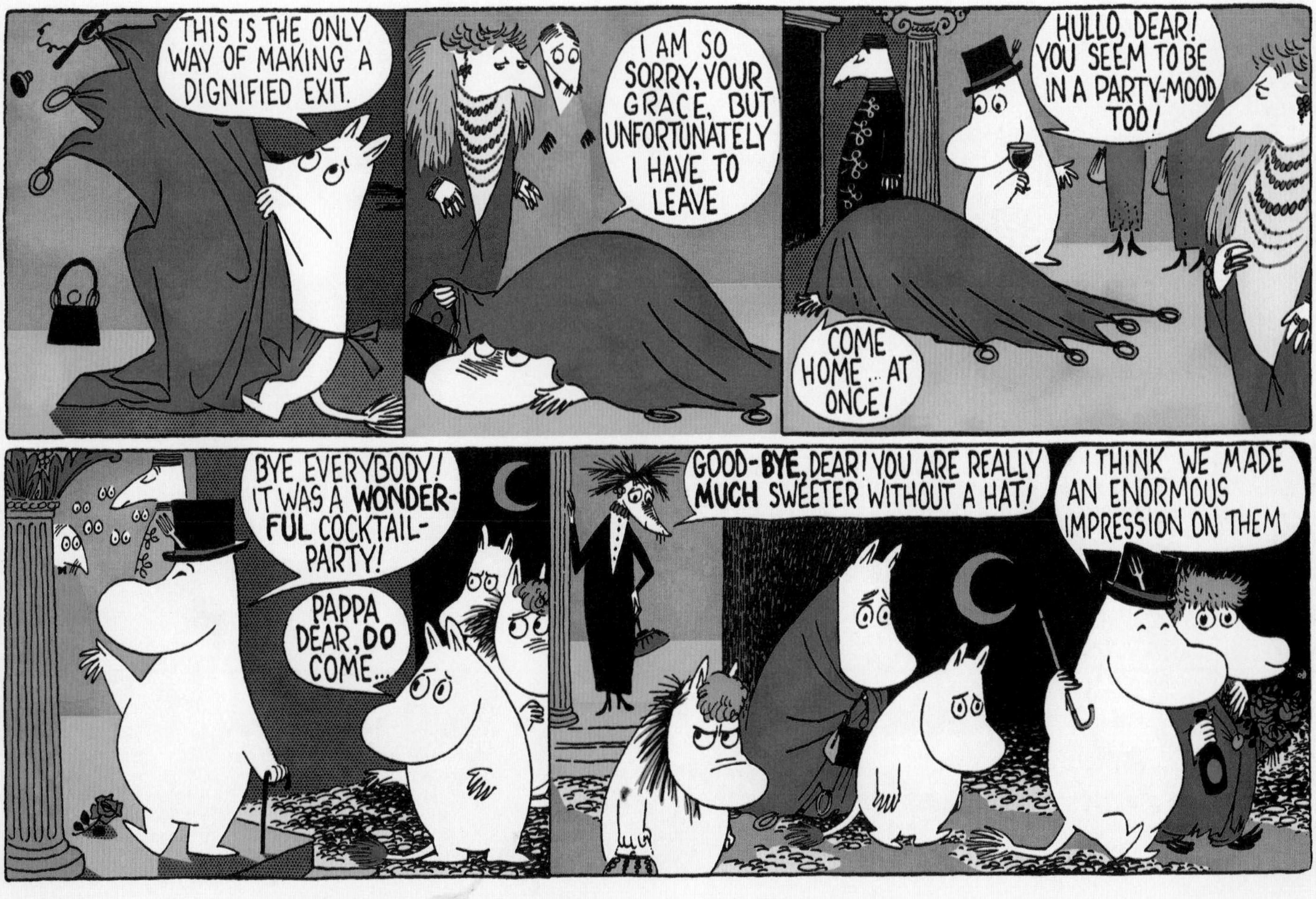
THIS IS THE ONLY WAY OF MAKING A DIGNIFIED EXIT.
I AM SO SORRY, YOUR GRACE, BUT UNFORTUNATELY I HAVE TO LEAVE
HULLO, DEAR! YOU SEEM TO BE IN A PARTY-MOOD TOO!
COME HOME ... AT ONCE!
BYE EVERYBODY! IT WAS A **WONDERFUL** COCKTAIL-PARTY!
PAPPA DEAR, **DO** COME...
GOOD-**BYE**, DEAR! YOU ARE REALLY **MUCH** SWEETER WITHOUT A HAT!
I THINK WE MADE AN ENORMOUS IMPRESSION ON THEM

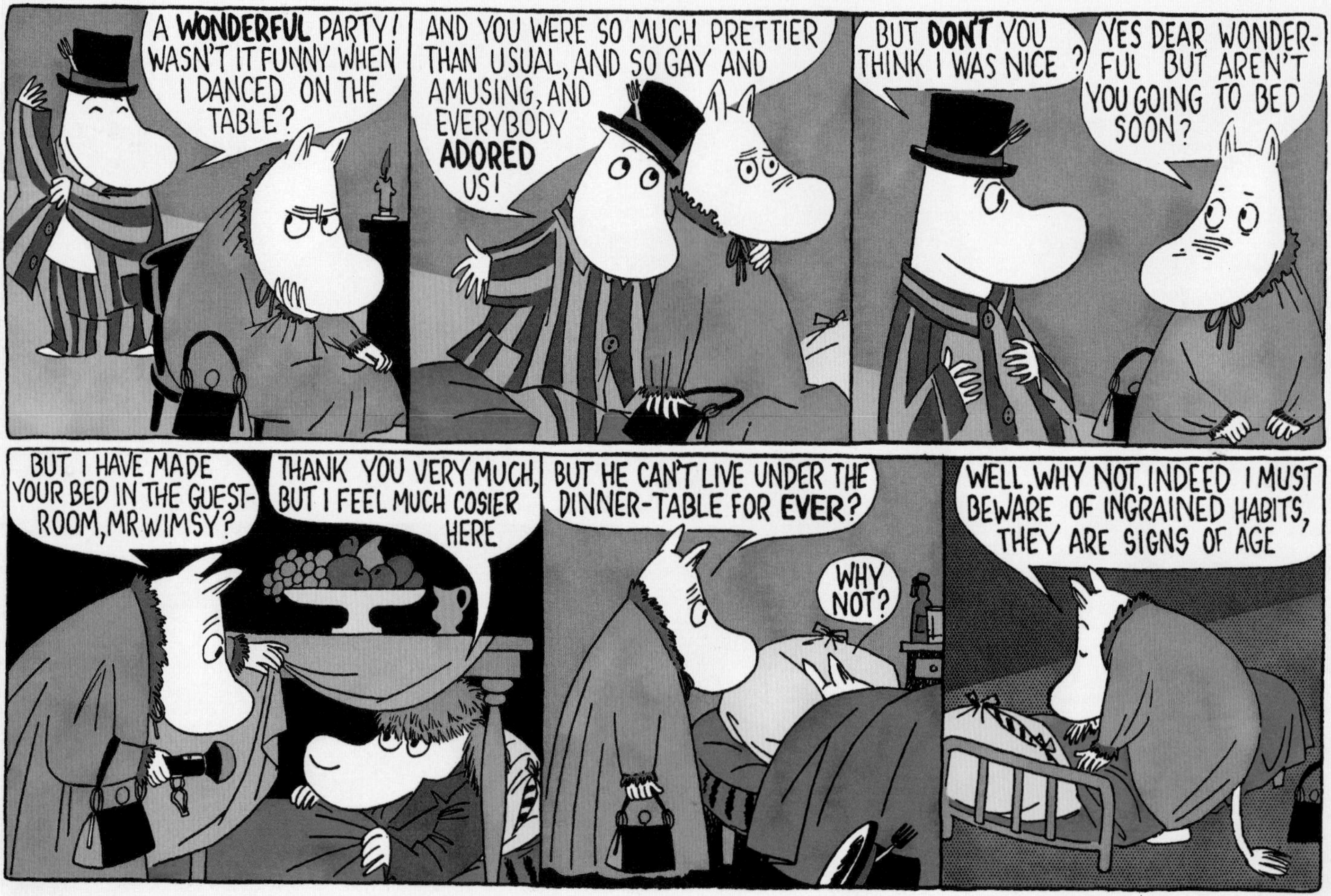
A **WONDERFUL** PARTY! WASN'T IT FUNNY WHEN I DANCED ON THE TABLE?
AND YOU WERE SO MUCH PRETTIER THAN USUAL, AND SO GAY AND AMUSING, AND EVERYBODY **ADORED** US!
BUT **DON'T** YOU THINK I WAS NICE?
YES DEAR WONDERFUL BUT AREN'T YOU GOING TO BED SOON?
BUT I HAVE MADE YOUR BED IN THE GUEST-ROOM, MR WIMSY?
THANK YOU VERY MUCH, BUT I FEEL MUCH COSIER HERE
BUT HE CAN'T LIVE UNDER THE DINNER-TABLE FOR **EVER**?
WHY NOT?
WELL, WHY NOT, INDEED I MUST BEWARE OF INGRAINED HABITS, THEY ARE SIGNS OF AGE

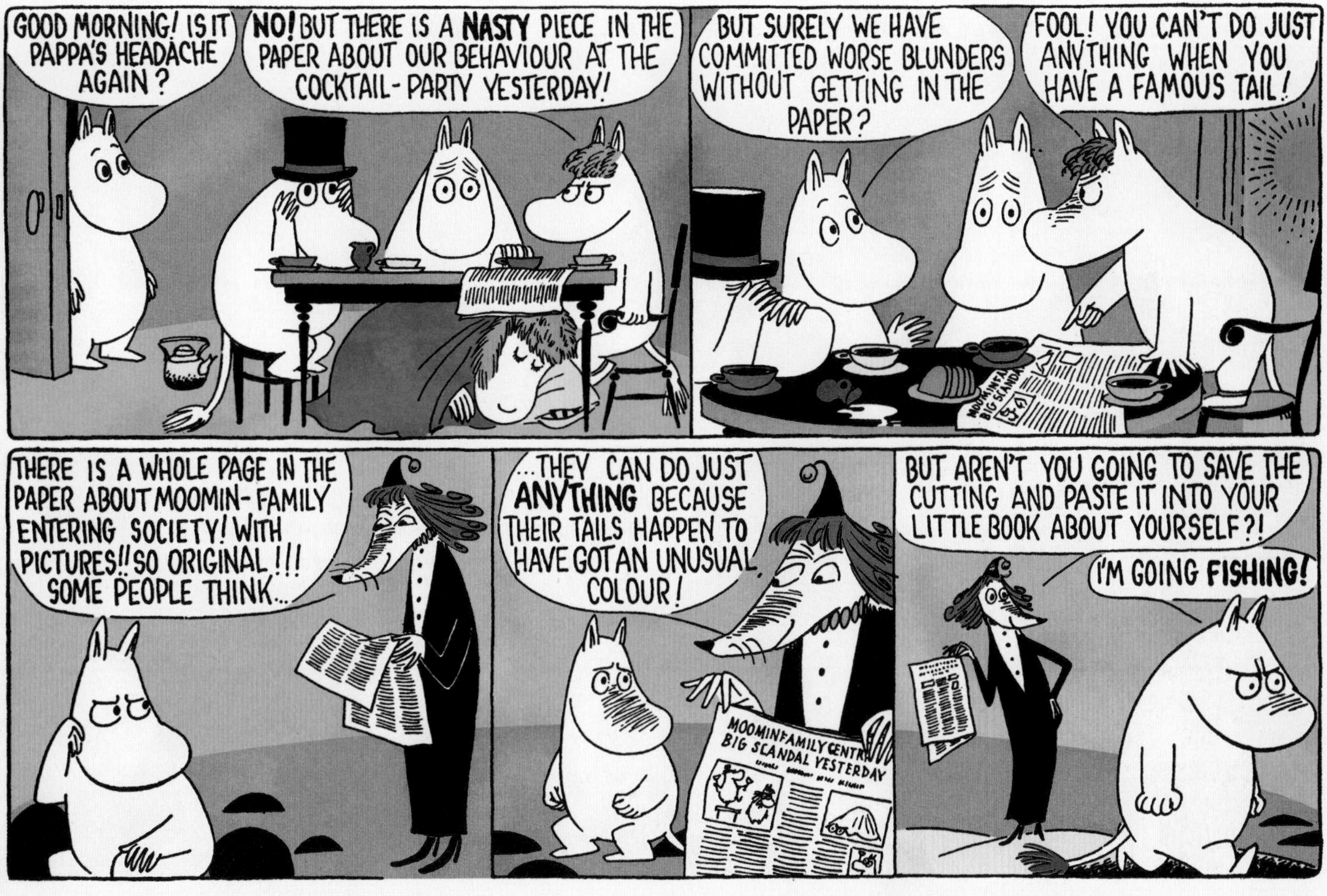
GOOD MORNING! IS IT PAPPA'S HEADACHE AGAIN?
NO! BUT THERE IS A NASTY PIECE IN THE PAPER ABOUT OUR BEHAVIOUR AT THE COCKTAIL-PARTY YESTERDAY!
BUT SURELY WE HAVE COMMITTED WORSE BLUNDERS WITHOUT GETTING IN THE PAPER?
FOOL! YOU CAN'T DO JUST ANYTHING WHEN YOU HAVE A FAMOUS TAIL!
THERE IS A WHOLE PAGE IN THE PAPER ABOUT MOOMIN-FAMILY ENTERING SOCIETY! WITH PICTURES!! SO ORIGINAL!!! SOME PEOPLE THINK...
...THEY CAN DO JUST ANYTHING BECAUSE THEIR TAILS HAPPEN TO HAVE GOT AN UNUSUAL COLOUR!
MOOMINFAMILY CENTR BIG SCANDAL YESTERDAY
BUT AREN'T YOU GOING TO SAVE THE CUTTING AND PASTE IT INTO YOUR LITTLE BOOK ABOUT YOURSELF?!
I'M GOING FISHING!

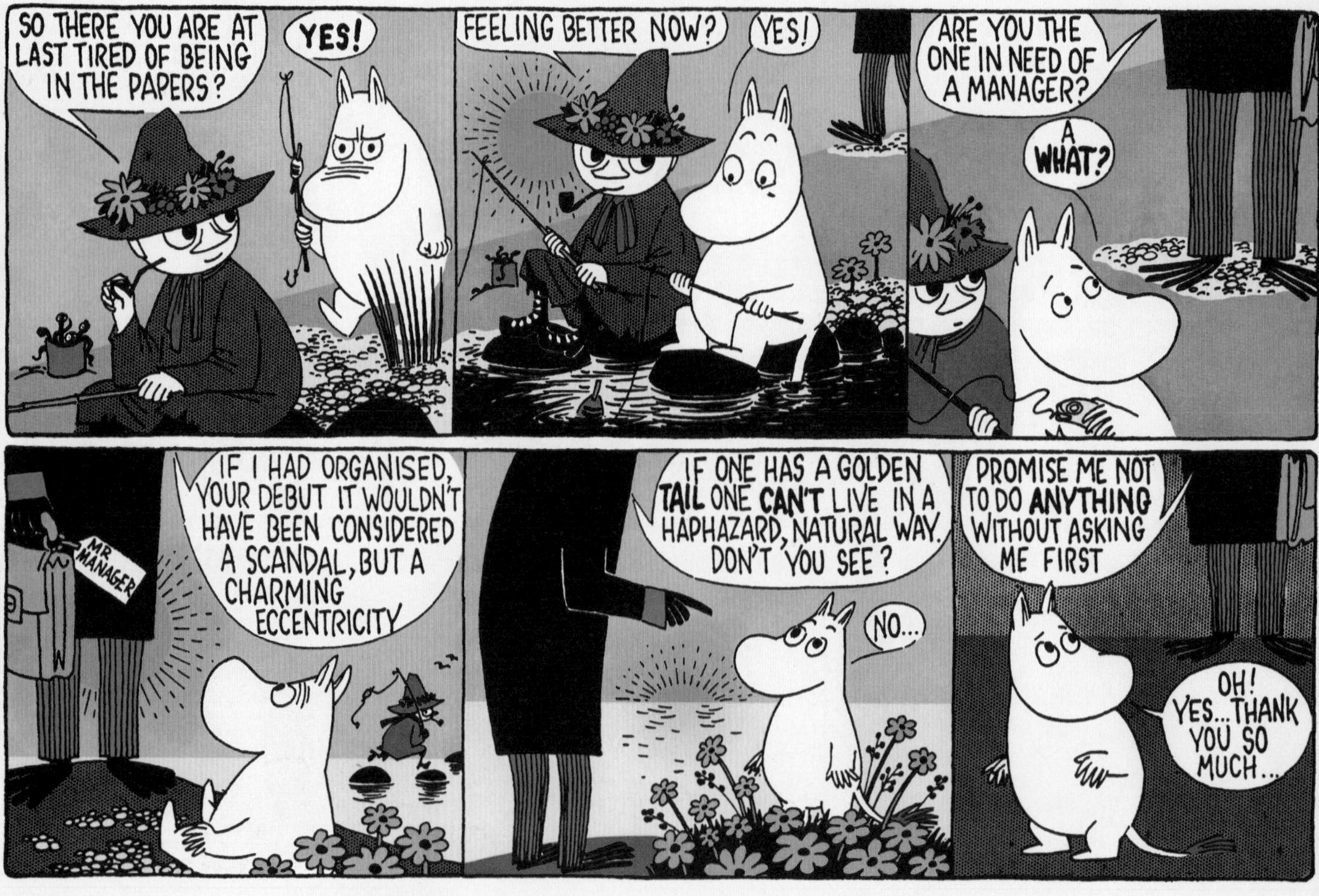
SO THERE YOU ARE AT LAST TIRED OF BEING IN THE PAPERS?
YES!
FEELING BETTER NOW?
YES!
ARE YOU THE ONE IN NEED OF A MANAGER?
A WHAT?
MR MANAGER
IF I HAD ORGANISED, YOUR DEBUT IT WOULDN'T HAVE BEEN CONSIDERED A SCANDAL, BUT A CHARMING ECCENTRICITY
IF ONE HAS A GOLDEN TAIL ONE CAN'T LIVE IN A HAPHAZARD, NATURAL WAY. DON'T YOU SEE?
NO...
PROMISE ME NOT TO DO ANYTHING WITHOUT ASKING ME FIRST
OH! YES... THANK YOU SO MUCH...

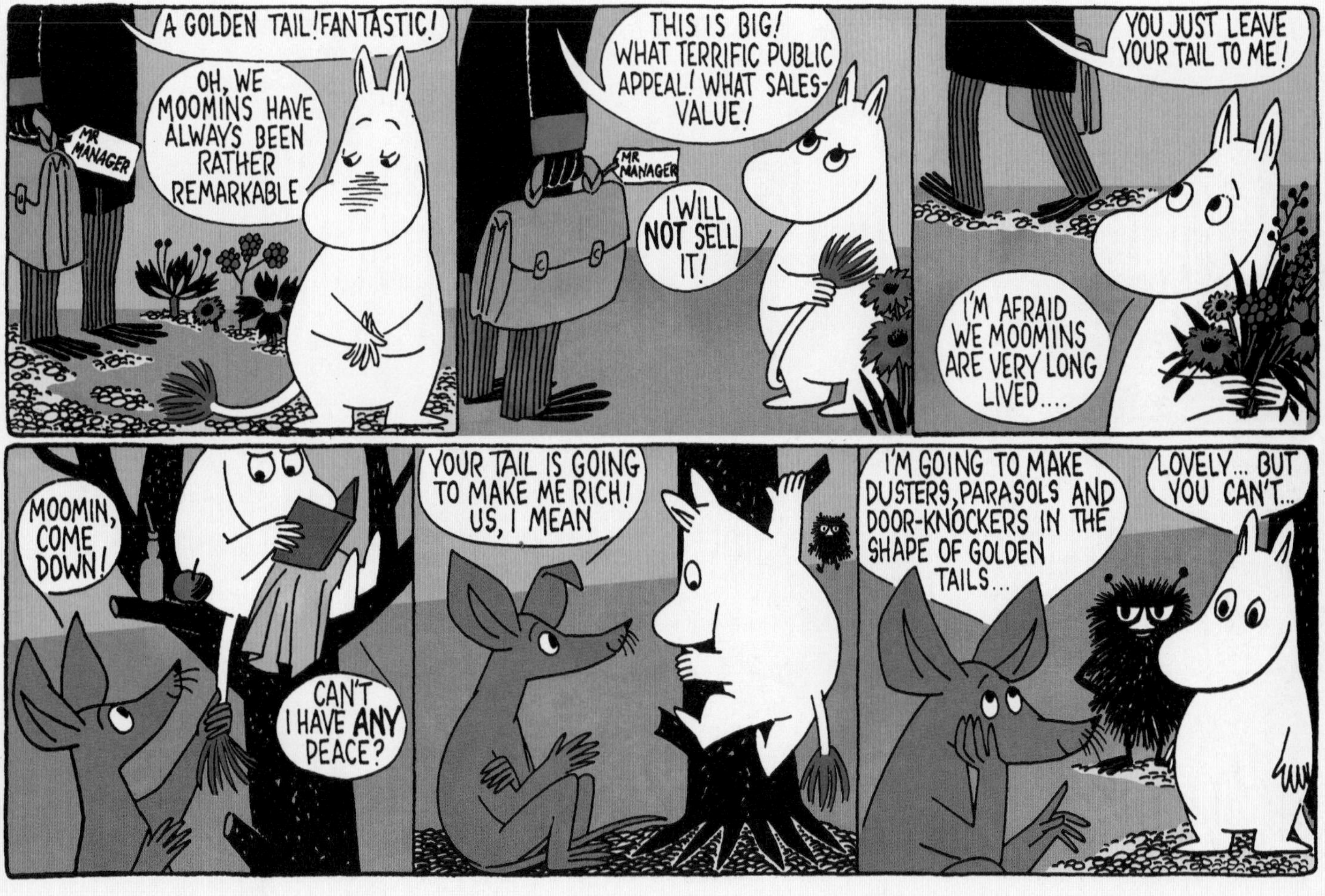
A GOLDEN TAIL! FANTASTIC!
OH, WE MOOMINS HAVE ALWAYS BEEN RATHER REMARKABLE
MR MANAGER
THIS IS BIG! WHAT TERRIFIC PUBLIC APPEAL! WHAT SALES-VALUE!
MR MANAGER
I WILL NOT SELL IT!
YOU JUST LEAVE YOUR TAIL TO ME!
I'M AFRAID WE MOOMINS ARE VERY LONG LIVED....
MOOMIN, COME DOWN!
CAN'T I HAVE ANY PEACE?
YOUR TAIL IS GOING TO MAKE ME RICH! US, I MEAN
I'M GOING TO MAKE DUSTERS, PARASOLS AND DOOR-KNOCKERS IN THE SHAPE OF GOLDEN TAILS...
LOVELY... BUT YOU CAN'T...

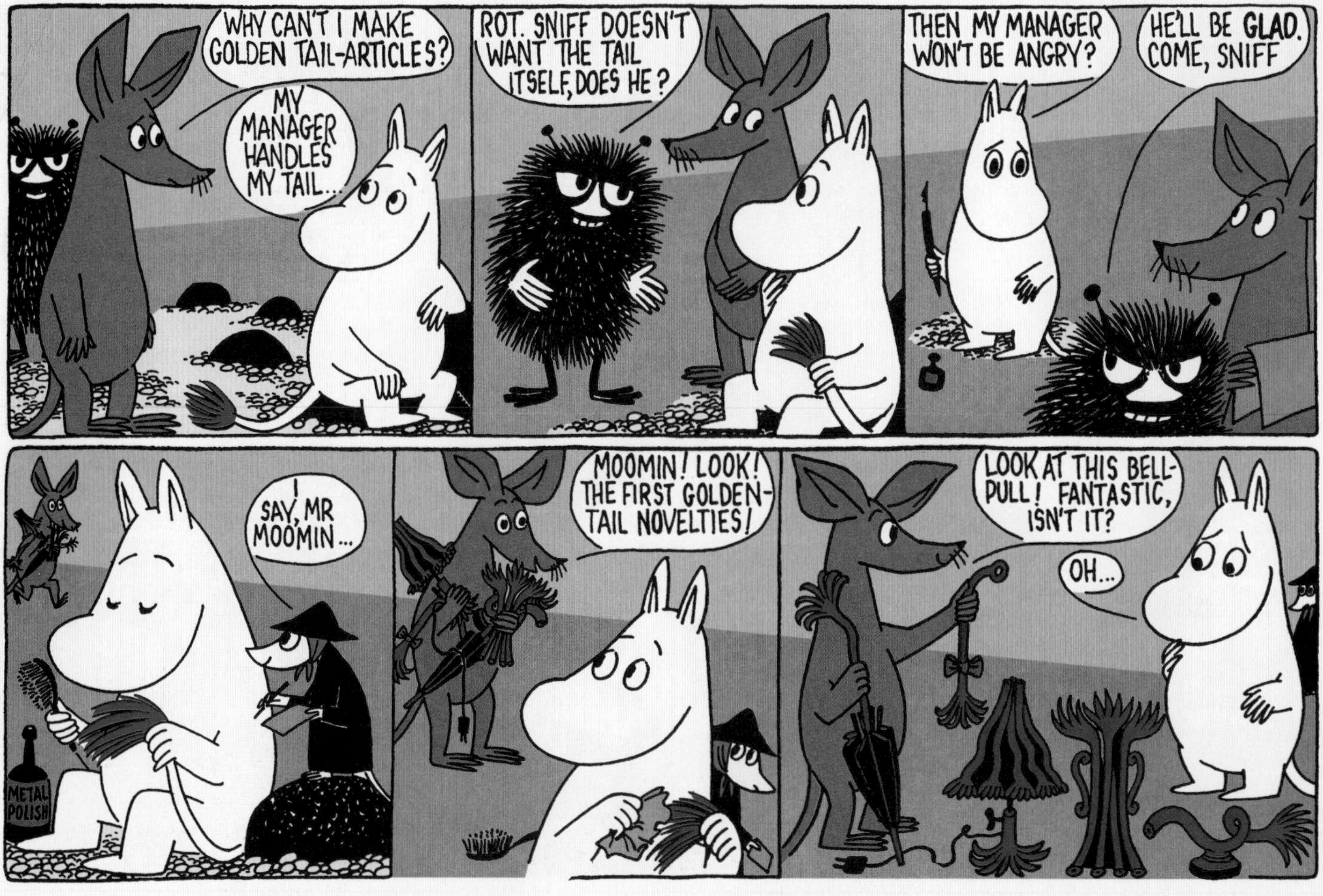
WHY CAN'T I MAKE GOLDEN TAIL-ARTICLES?
MY MANAGER HANDLES MY TAIL...
ROT. SNIFF DOESN'T WANT THE TAIL ITSELF, DOES HE?
THEN MY MANAGER WON'T BE ANGRY?
HE'LL BE GLAD. COME, SNIFF
I SAY, MR MOOMIN...
METAL POLISH
MOOMIN! LOOK! THE FIRST GOLDEN-TAIL NOVELTIES!
LOOK AT THIS BELL-PULL! FANTASTIC, ISN'T IT?
OH...

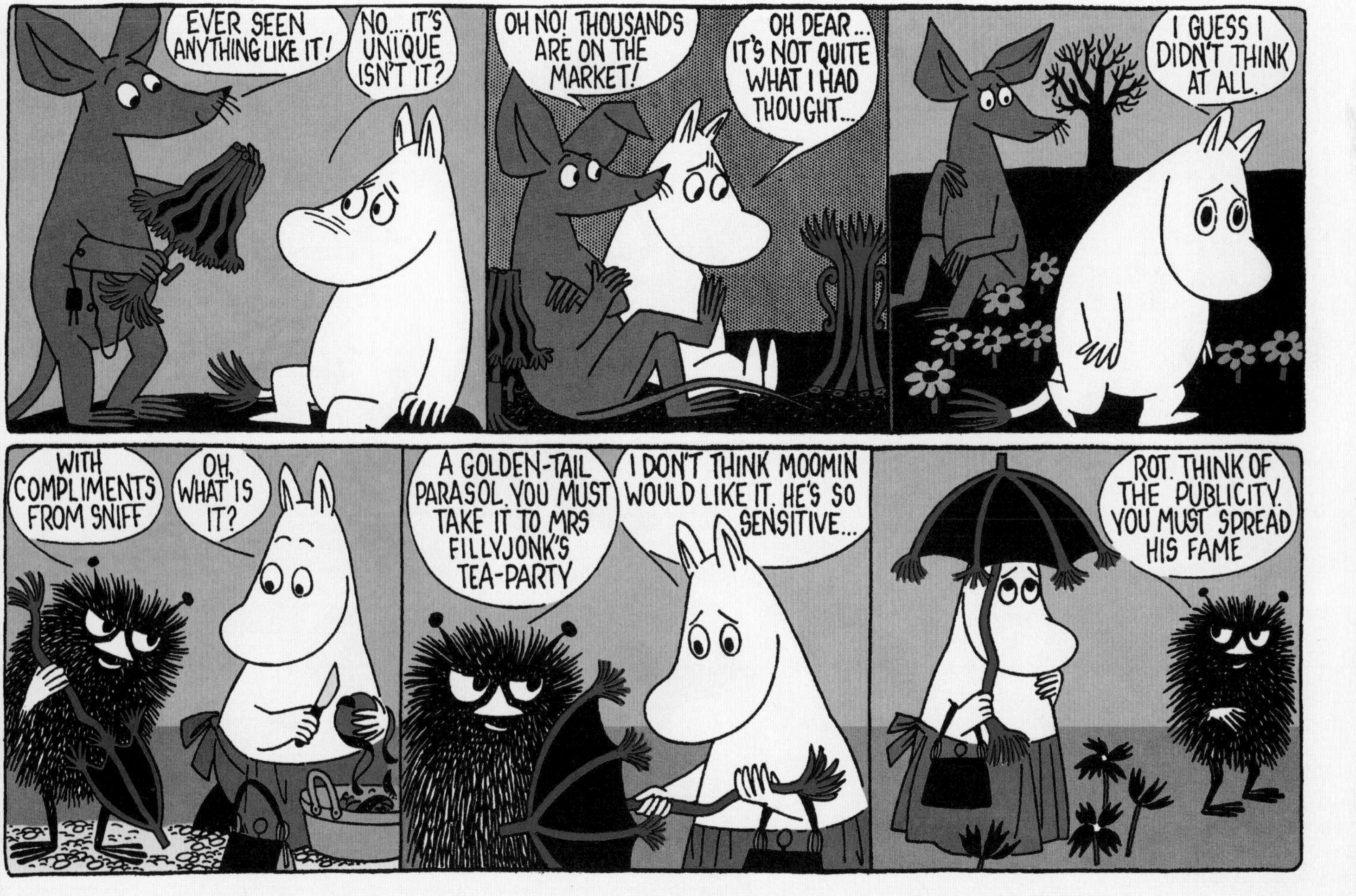
EVER SEEN ANYTHING LIKE IT!
NO.... IT'S UNIQUE ISN'T IT?
OH NO! THOUSANDS ARE ON THE MARKET!
OH DEAR... IT'S NOT QUITE WHAT I HAD THOUGHT...
I GUESS I DIDN'T THINK AT ALL.
WITH COMPLIMENTS FROM SNIFF
OH, WHAT IS IT?
A GOLDEN-TAIL PARASOL. YOU MUST TAKE IT TO MRS FILLYJONK'S TEA-PARTY
I DON'T THINK MOOMIN WOULD LIKE IT. HE'S SO SENSITIVE...
ROT. THINK OF THE PUBLICITY. YOU MUST SPREAD HIS FAME

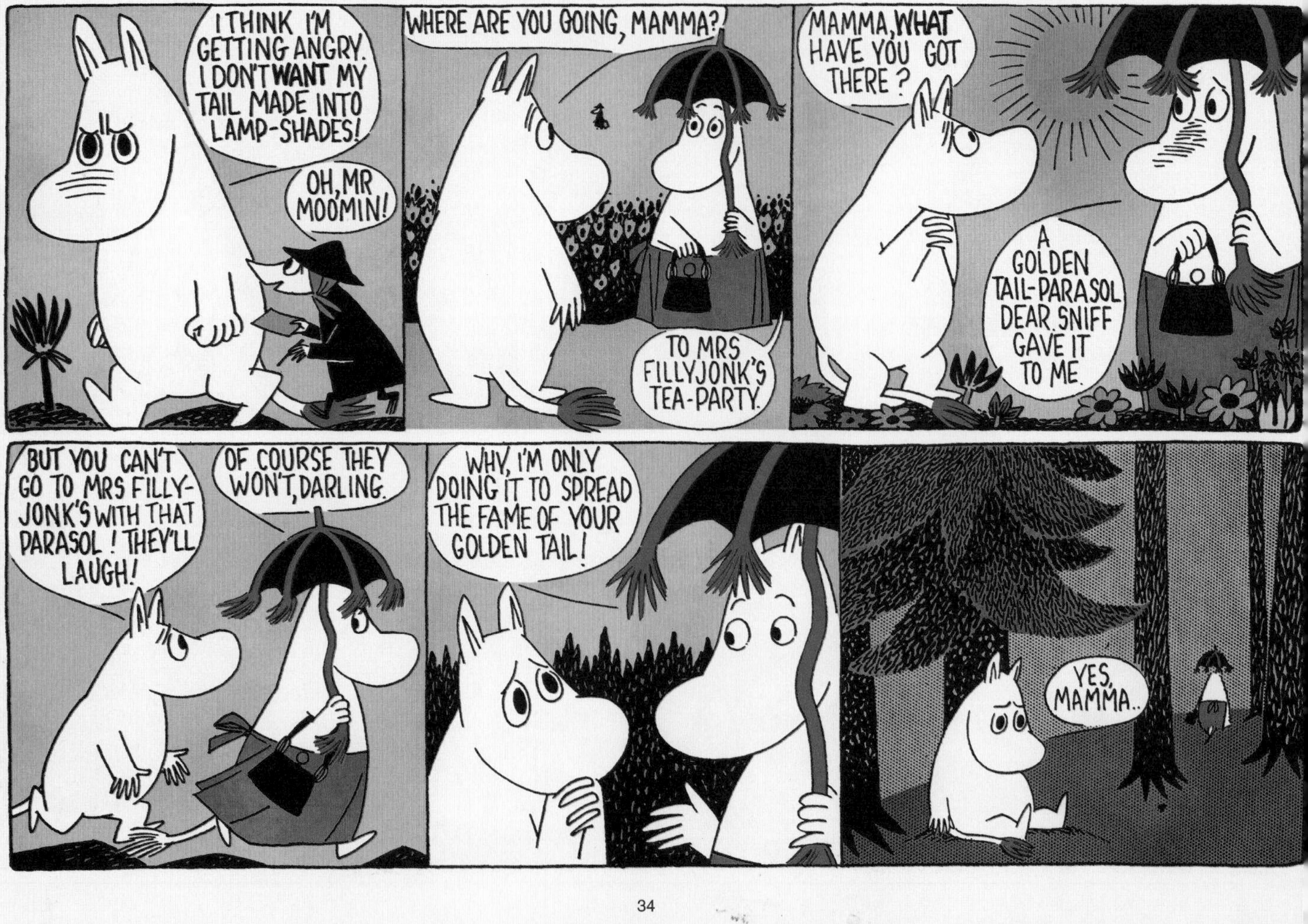
I THINK I'M GETTING ANGRY. I DON'T WANT MY TAIL MADE INTO LAMP-SHADES!
OH, MR MOOMIN!
WHERE ARE YOU GOING, MAMMA?
TO MRS FILLYJONK'S TEA-PARTY.
MAMMA, WHAT HAVE YOU GOT THERE ?
A GOLDEN TAIL-PARASOL DEAR. SNIFF GAVE IT TO ME.
BUT YOU CAN'T GO TO MRS FILLY-JONK'S WITH THAT PARASOL ! THEY'LL LAUGH!
OF COURSE THEY WON'T, DARLING.
WHY, I'M ONLY DOING IT TO SPREAD THE FAME OF YOUR GOLDEN TAIL!
YES, MAMMA..

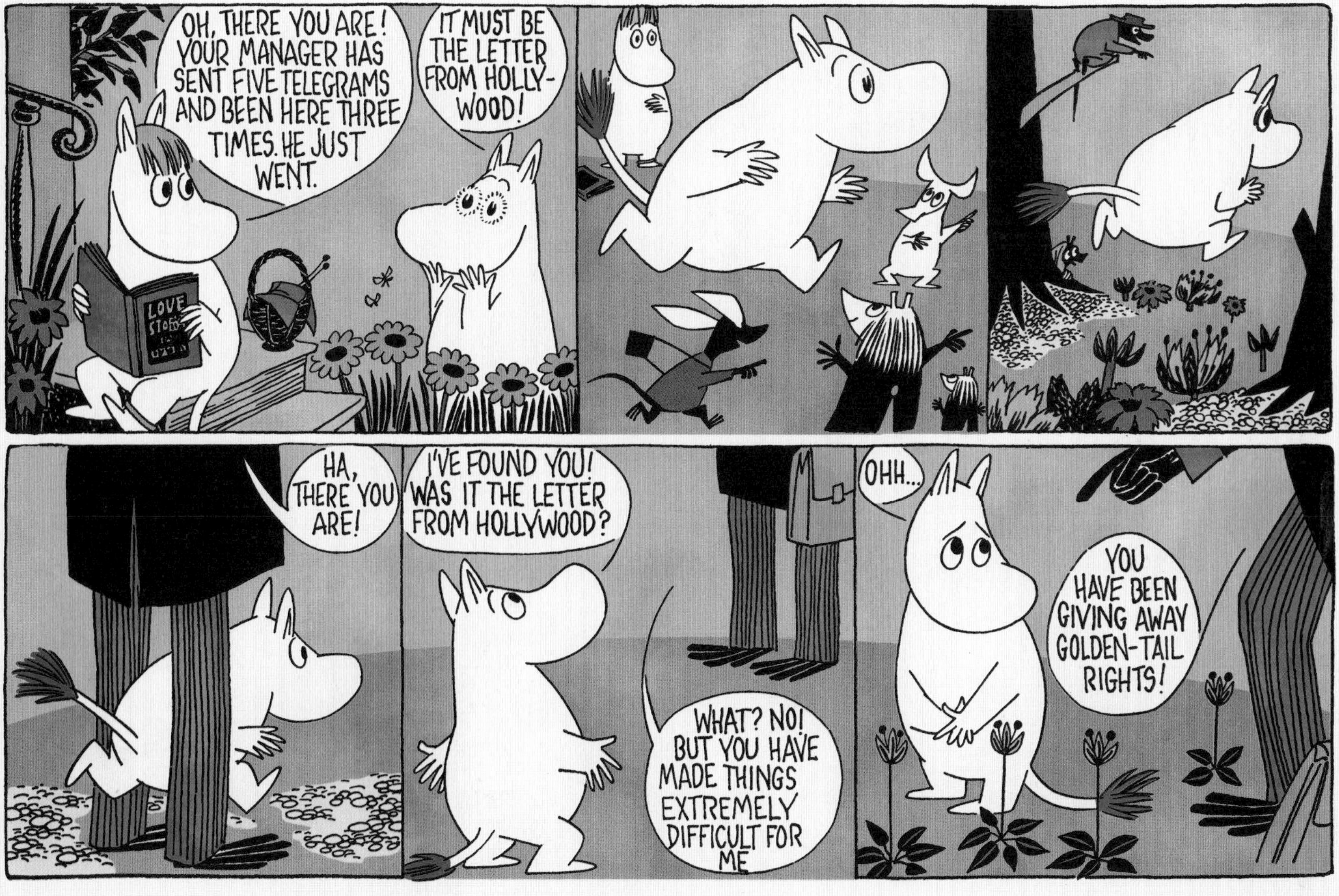
OH, THERE YOU ARE! YOUR MANAGER HAS SENT FIVE TELEGRAMS AND BEEN HERE THREE TIMES. HE JUST WENT.
IT MUST BE THE LETTER FROM HOLLY-WOOD!
LOVE
HA, THERE YOU ARE!
I'VE FOUND YOU! WAS IT THE LETTER FROM HOLLYWOOD?
WHAT? NO! BUT YOU HAVE MADE THINGS EXTREMELY DIFFICULT FOR ME
OHH...
YOU HAVE BEEN GIVING AWAY GOLDEN-TAIL RIGHTS!

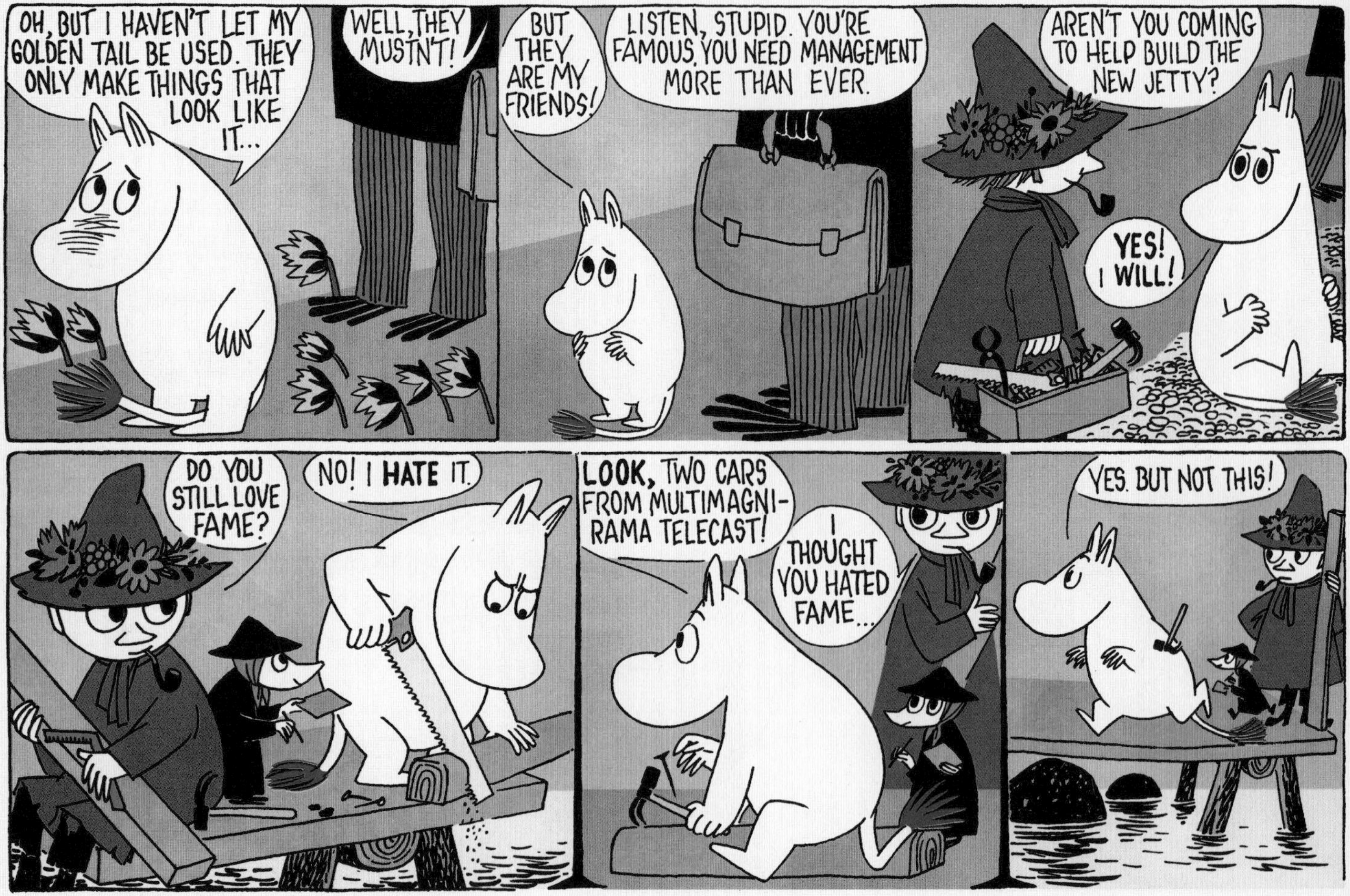

OH, BUT I HAVEN'T LET MY GOLDEN TAIL BE USED. THEY ONLY MAKE THINGS THAT LOOK LIKE IT...
WELL, THEY MUSTN'T!
BUT THEY ARE MY FRIENDS!
LISTEN, STUPID. YOU'RE FAMOUS. YOU NEED MANAGEMENT MORE THAN EVER.
AREN'T YOU COMING TO HELP BUILD THE NEW JETTY?
YES! I WILL!
DO YOU STILL LOVE FAME?
NO! I HATE IT.
LOOK, TWO CARS FROM MULTIMAGNI-RAMA TELECAST!
I THOUGHT YOU HATED FAME...
YES. BUT NOT THIS!

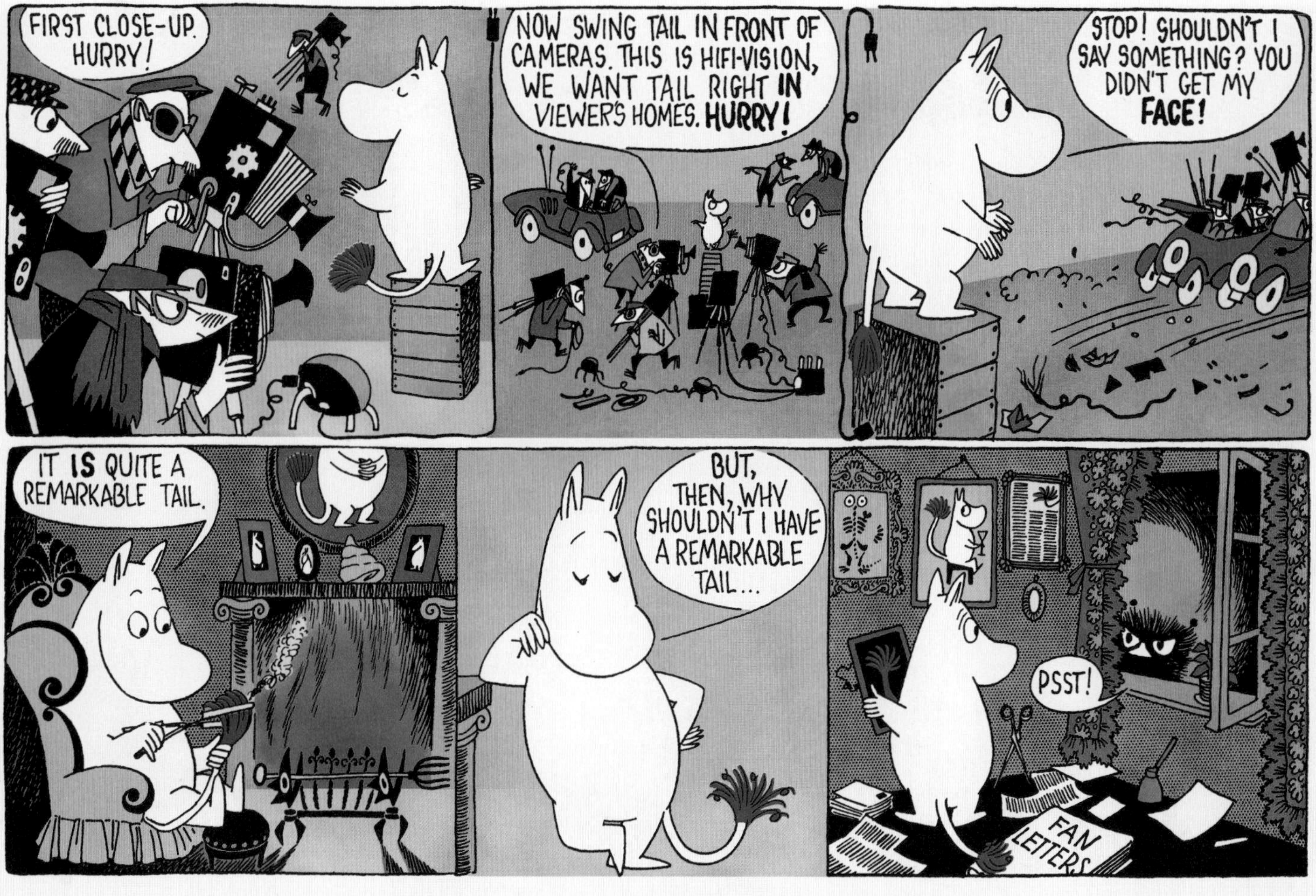
FIRST CLOSE-UP. HURRY!
NOW SWING TAIL IN FRONT OF CAMERAS. THIS IS HIFI-VISION, WE WANT TAIL RIGHT **IN** VIEWER'S HOMES. **HURRY!**
STOP! SHOULDN'T I SAY SOMETHING? YOU DIDN'T GET MY **FACE!**
IT **IS** QUITE A REMARKABLE TAIL.
BUT, THEN, WHY SHOULDN'T I HAVE A REMARKABLE TAIL...
PSST!
FAN LETTERS

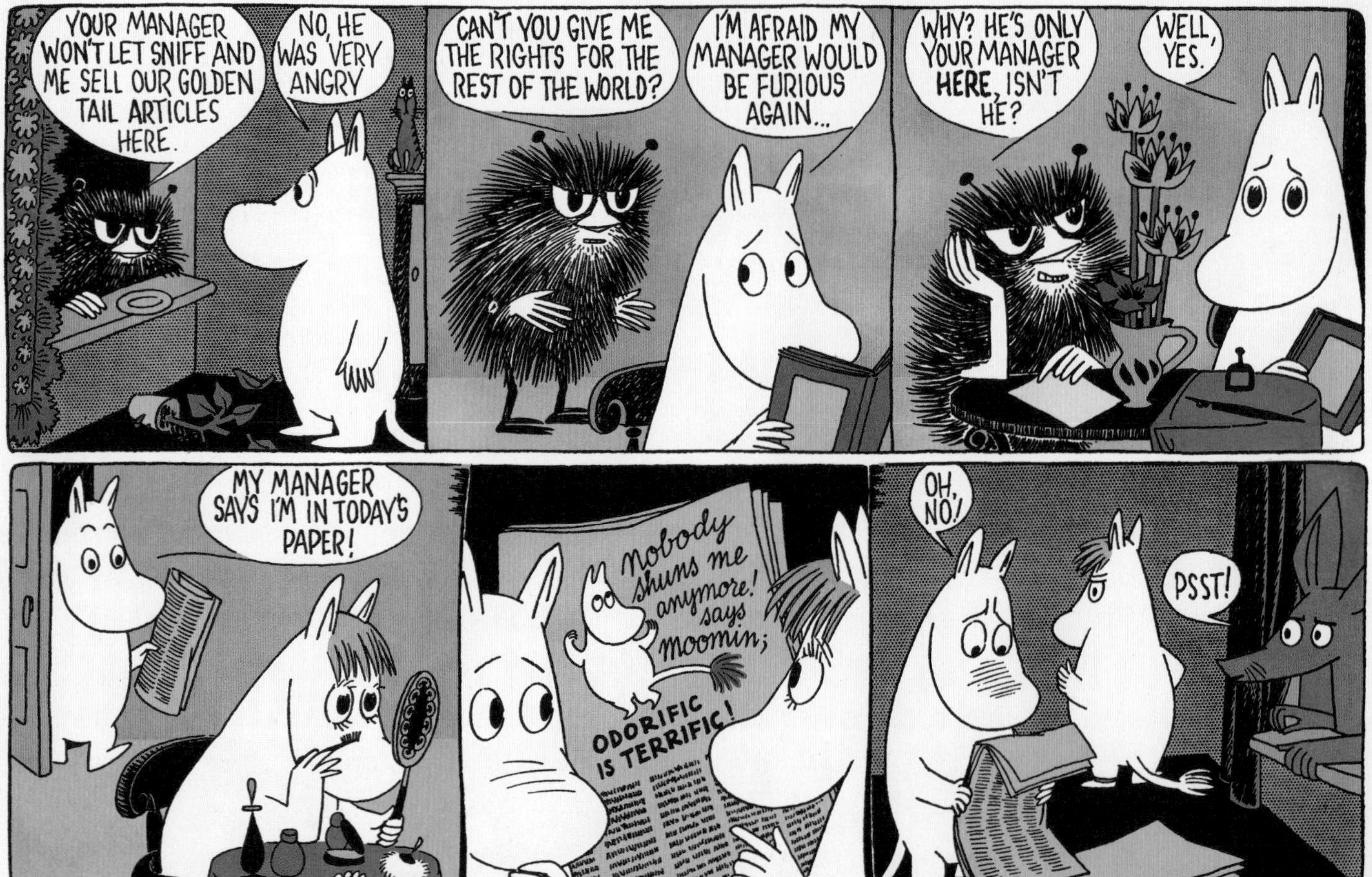
YOUR MANAGER WON'T LET SNIFF AND ME SELL OUR GOLDEN TAIL ARTICLES HERE.
NO, HE WAS VERY ANGRY
CAN'T YOU GIVE ME THE RIGHTS FOR THE REST OF THE WORLD?
I'M AFRAID MY MANAGER WOULD BE FURIOUS AGAIN...
WHY? HE'S ONLY YOUR MANAGER HERE, ISN'T HE?
WELL, YES.
MY MANAGER SAYS I'M IN TODAY'S PAPER!
nobody shuns me anymore! says moomin;
ODORIFIC IS TERRIFIC!
OH, NO!
PSST!

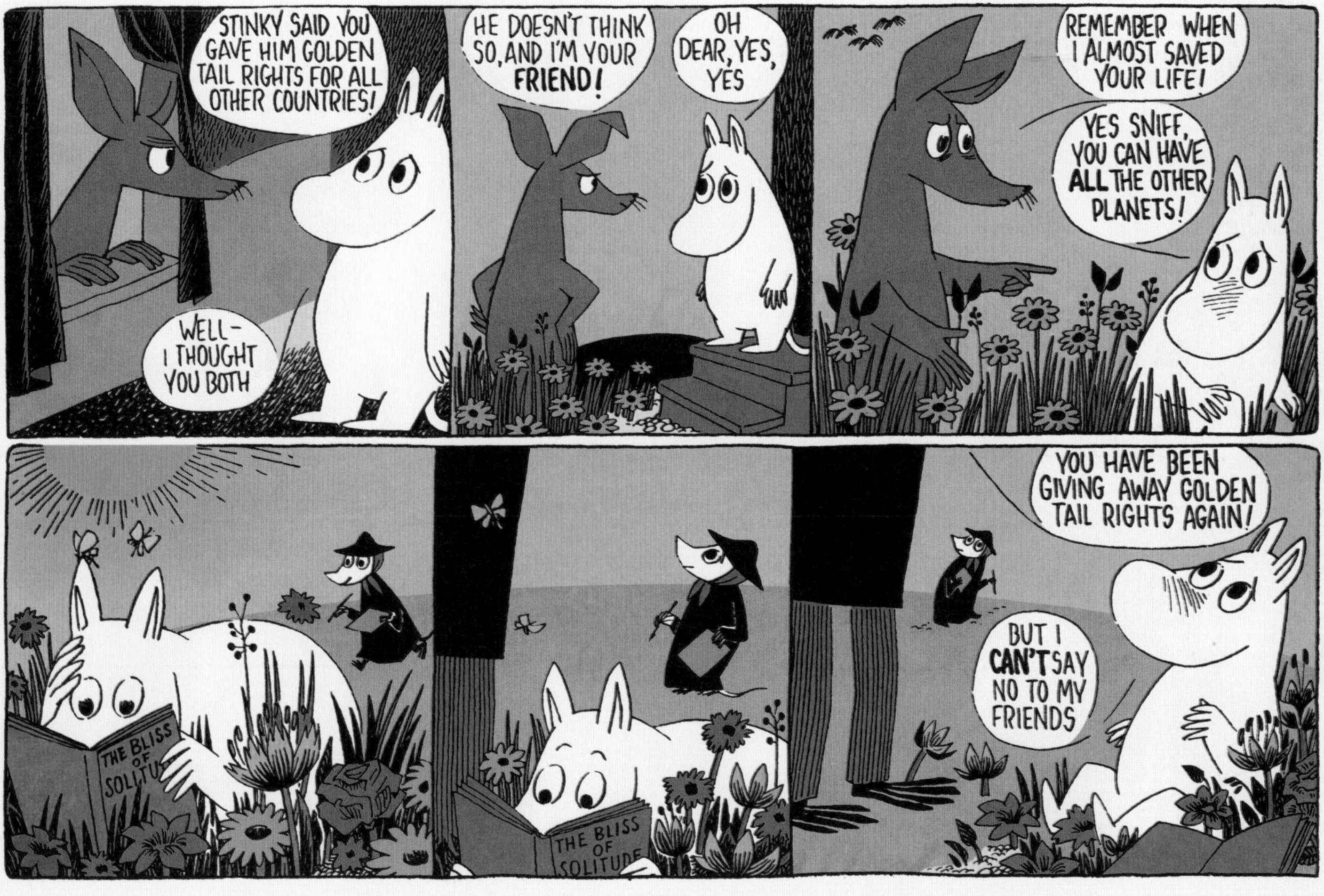
STINKY SAID YOU GAVE HIM GOLDEN TAIL RIGHTS FOR ALL OTHER COUNTRIES!
WELL- I THOUGHT YOU BOTH
HE DOESN'T THINK SO, AND I'M YOUR FRIEND!
OH DEAR, YES, YES
REMEMBER WHEN I ALMOST SAVED YOUR LIFE!
YES SNIFF, YOU CAN HAVE ALL THE OTHER PLANETS!
THE BLISS OF SOLITU
THE BLISS OF SOLITUDE
YOU HAVE BEEN GIVING AWAY GOLDEN TAIL RIGHTS AGAIN!
BUT I CAN'T SAY NO TO MY FRIENDS

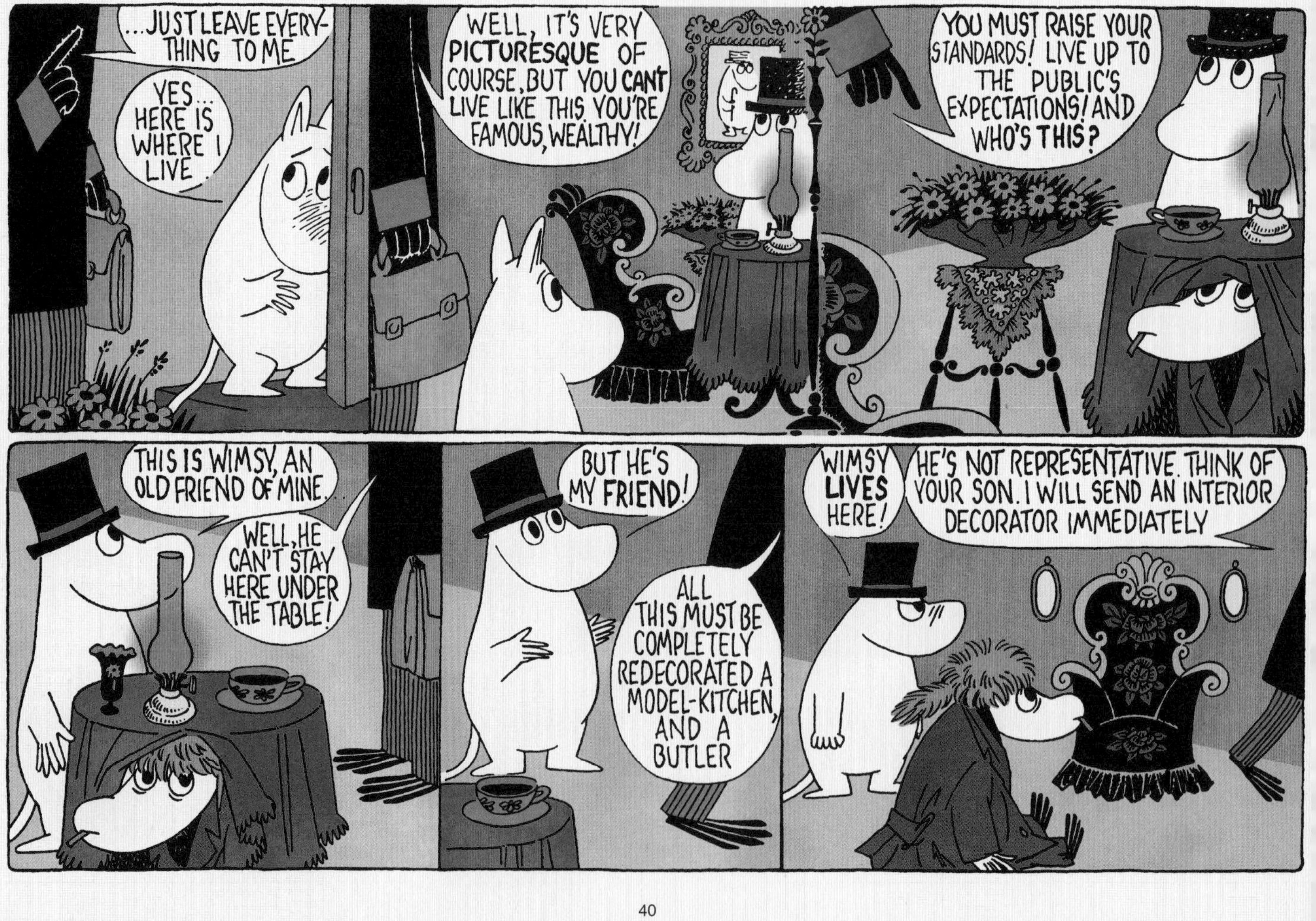
...JUST LEAVE EVERY-THING TO ME
YES... HERE IS WHERE I LIVE
WELL, IT'S VERY **PICTURESQUE** OF COURSE, BUT YOU **CAN'T** LIVE LIKE THIS YOU'RE FAMOUS, WEALTHY!
YOU MUST RAISE YOUR STANDARDS! LIVE UP TO THE PUBLIC'S EXPECTATIONS! AND WHO'S **THIS**?
THIS IS WIMSY, AN OLD FRIEND OF MINE...
WELL, HE CAN'T STAY HERE UNDER THE TABLE!
BUT HE'S MY **FRIEND**!
ALL THIS MUST BE COMPLETELY REDECORATED A MODEL-KITCHEN, AND A BUTLER
WIMSY **LIVES** HERE!
HE'S NOT REPRESENTATIVE. THINK OF YOUR SON. I WILL SEND AN INTERIOR DECORATOR IMMEDIATELY

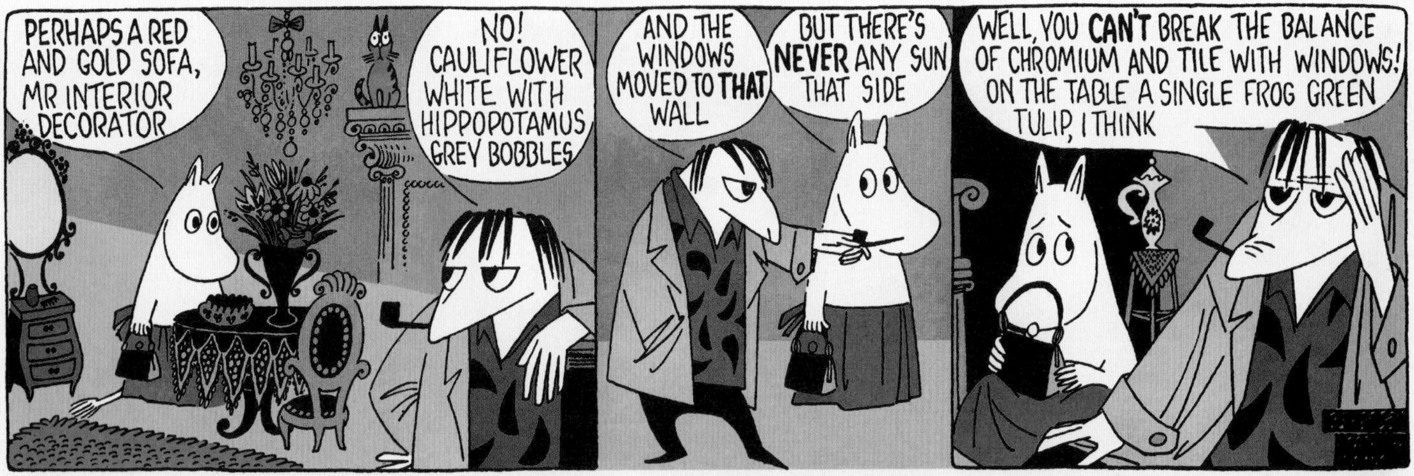
PERHAPS A RED AND GOLD SOFA, MR INTERIOR DECORATOR
NO! CAULIFLOWER WHITE WITH HIPPOPOTAMUS GREY BOBBLES
AND THE WINDOWS MOVED TO THAT WALL
BUT THERE'S NEVER ANY SUN THAT SIDE
WELL, YOU CAN'T BREAK THE BALANCE OF CHROMIUM AND TILE WITH WINDOWS! ON THE TABLE A SINGLE FROG GREEN TULIP, I THINK

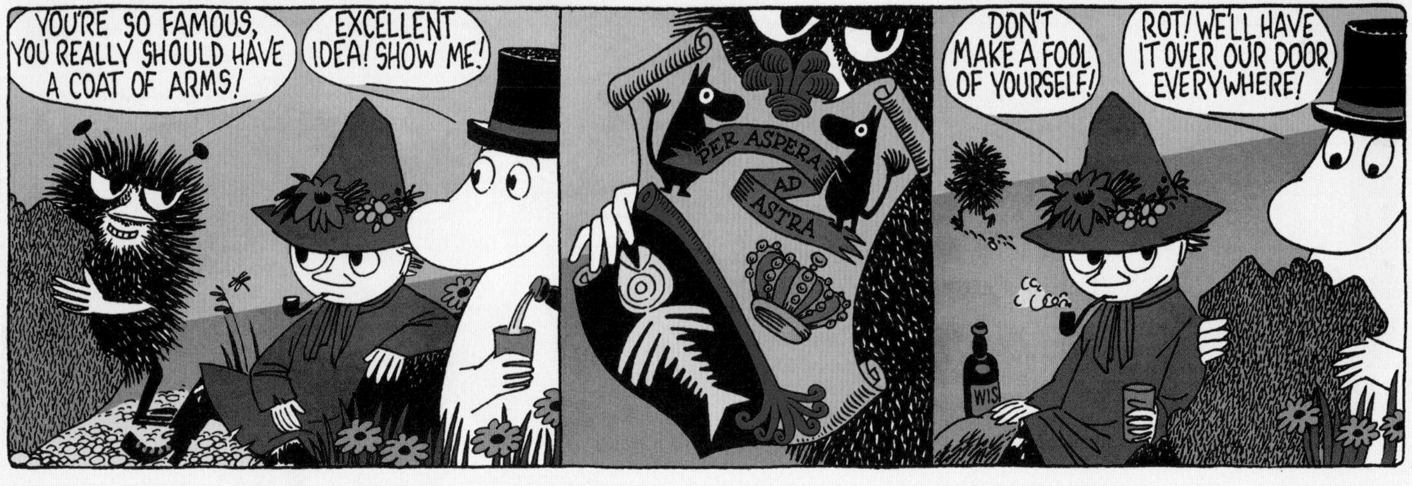
YOU'RE SO FAMOUS, YOU REALLY SHOULD HAVE A COAT OF ARMS!
EXCELLENT IDEA! SHOW ME!
PER ASPERA AD ASTRA
DON'T MAKE A FOOL OF YOURSELF!
ROT! WE'LL HAVE IT OVER OUR DOOR, EVERYWHERE!
WIS

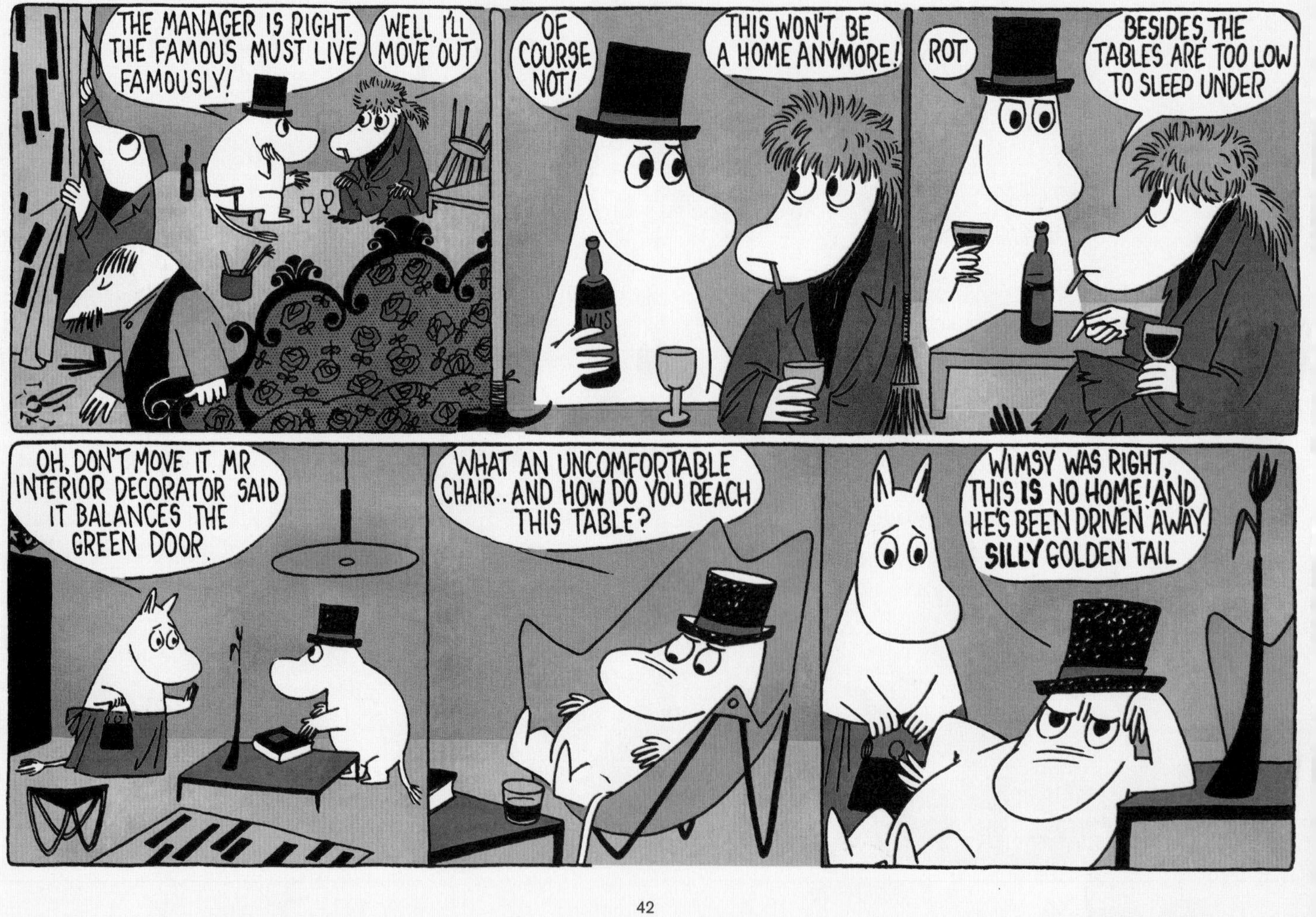
THE MANAGER IS RIGHT. THE FAMOUS MUST LIVE FAMOUSLY!
WELL, I'LL MOVE OUT
OF COURSE NOT!
THIS WON'T BE A HOME ANYMORE!
ROT
BESIDES, THE TABLES ARE TOO LOW TO SLEEP UNDER
OH, DON'T MOVE IT. MR INTERIOR DECORATOR SAID IT BALANCES THE GREEN DOOR.
WHAT AN UNCOMFORTABLE CHAIR.. AND HOW DO YOU REACH THIS TABLE?
WIMSY WAS RIGHT, THIS IS NO HOME! AND HE'S BEEN DRIVEN AWAY. SILLY GOLDEN TAIL

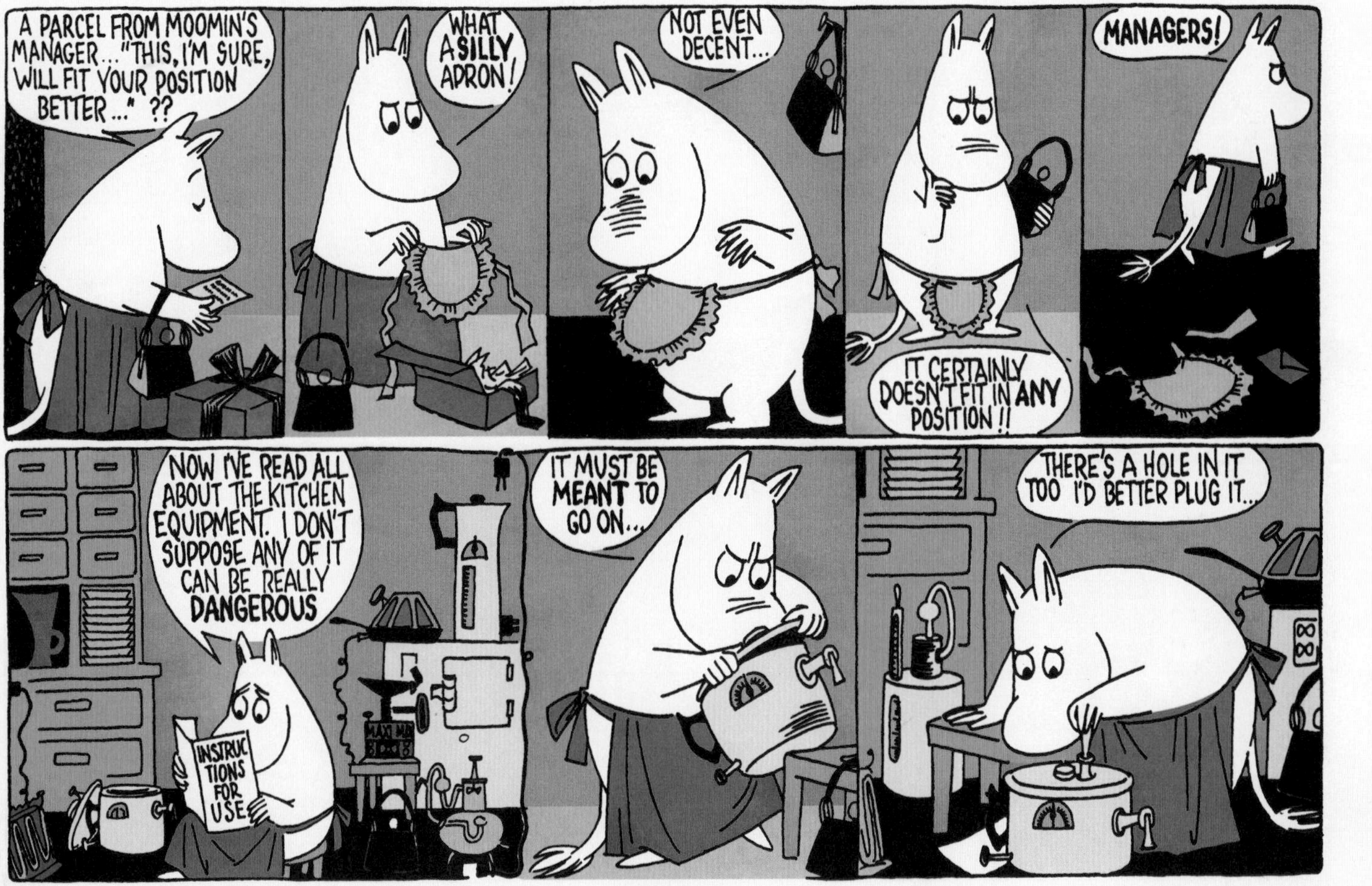
A PARCEL FROM MOOMIN'S MANAGER ... "THIS, I'M SURE, WILL FIT YOUR POSITION BETTER ..." ??
WHAT A SILLY APRON!
NOT EVEN DECENT ...
IT CERTAINLY DOESN'T FIT IN ANY POSITION !!
MANAGERS!
NOW I'VE READ ALL ABOUT THE KITCHEN EQUIPMENT. I DON'T SUPPOSE ANY OF IT CAN BE REALLY DANGEROUS
INSTRUCTIONS FOR USE
MAXI MA
IT MUST BE MEANT TO GO ON ...
THERE'S A HOLE IN IT TOO I'D BETTER PLUG IT ...

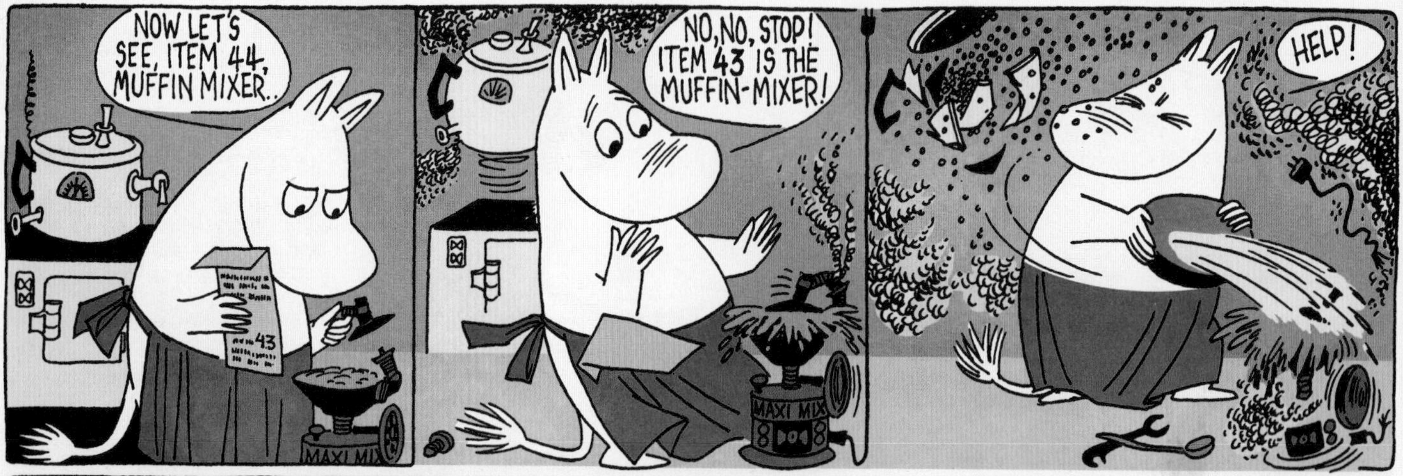
NOW LET'S SEE, ITEM 44, MUFFIN MIXER..
43
MAXI MIX
NO, NO, STOP! ITEM 43 IS THE MUFFIN-MIXER!
MAXI MIX
HELP!

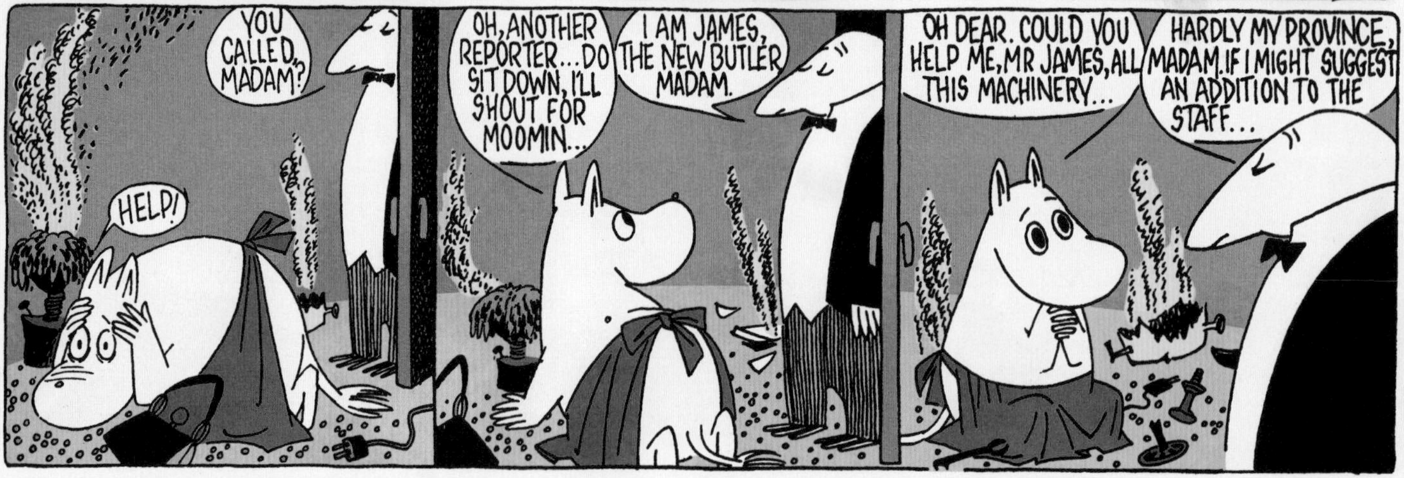
YOU CALLED, MADAM?
HELP!
OH, ANOTHER REPORTER... DO SIT DOWN, I'LL SHOUT FOR MOOMIN...
I AM JAMES, THE NEW BUTLER MADAM.
OH DEAR. COULD YOU HELP ME, MR JAMES, ALL THIS MACHINERY...
HARDLY MY PROVINCE, MADAM. IF I MIGHT SUGGEST AN ADDITION TO THE STAFF...

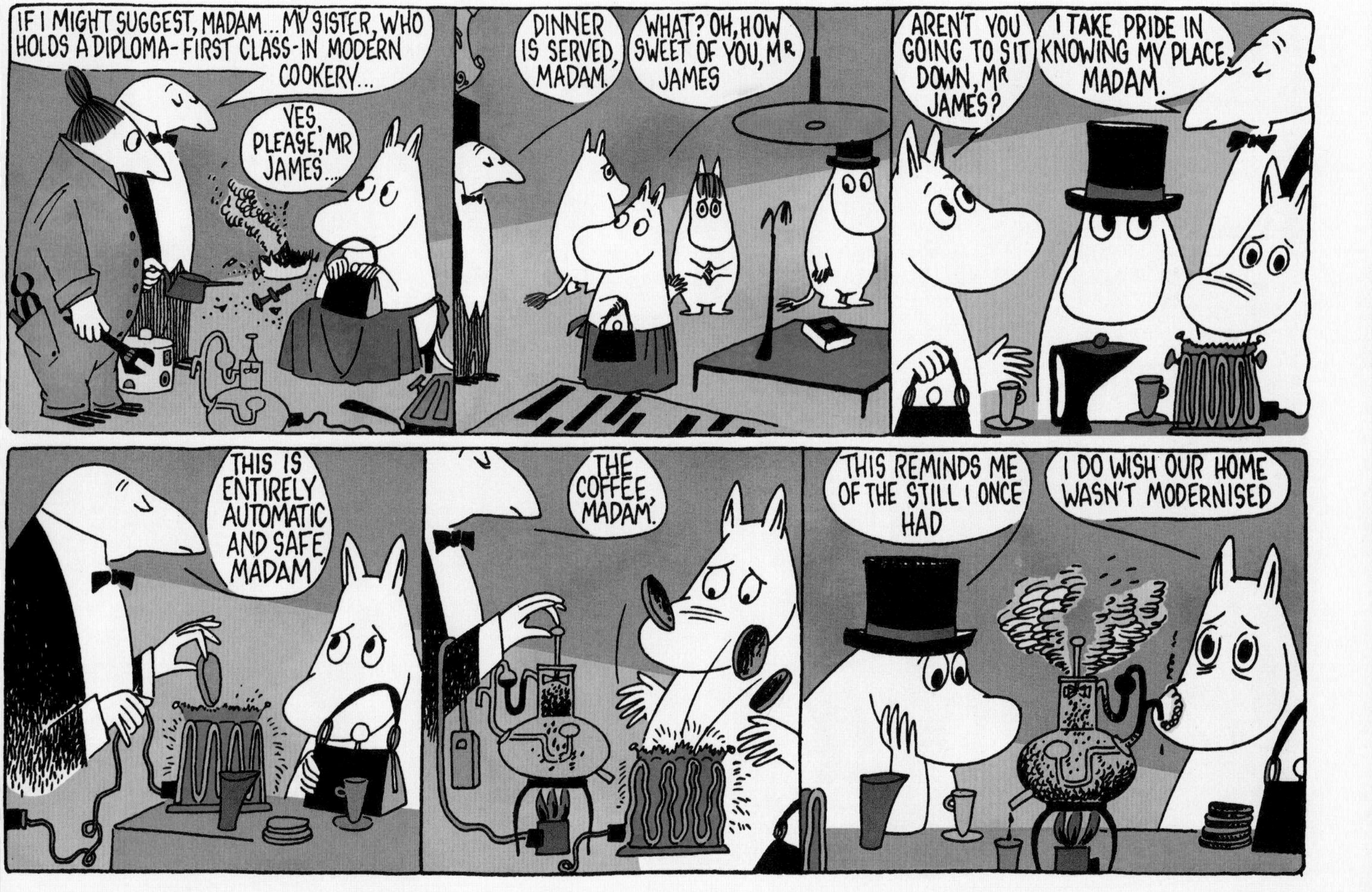
IF I MIGHT SUGGEST, MADAM... MY SISTER, WHO HOLDS A DIPLOMA- FIRST CLASS- IN MODERN COOKERY...
YES, PLEASE, MR JAMES....
DINNER IS SERVED, MADAM.
WHAT? OH, HOW SWEET OF YOU, MR JAMES
AREN'T YOU GOING TO SIT DOWN, MR JAMES?
I TAKE PRIDE IN KNOWING MY PLACE, MADAM.
THIS IS ENTIRELY AUTOMATIC AND SAFE, MADAM
THE COFFEE, MADAM.
THIS REMINDS ME OF THE STILL I ONCE HAD
I DO WISH OUR HOME WASN'T MODERNISED

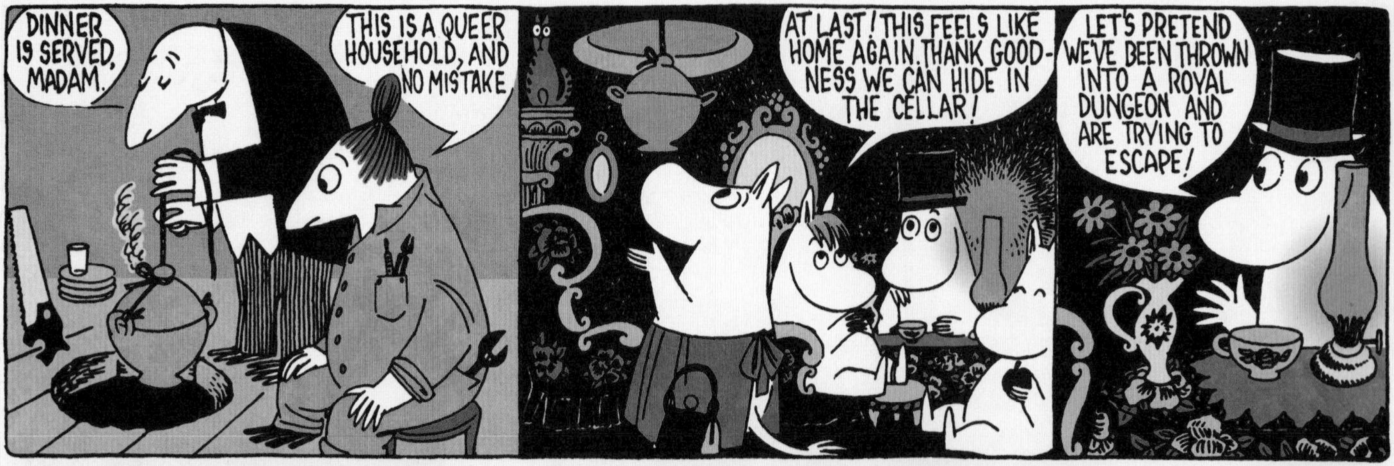
DINNER IS SERVED, MADAM.
THIS IS A QUEER HOUSEHOLD, AND NO MISTAKE
AT LAST! THIS FEELS LIKE HOME AGAIN. THANK GOODNESS WE CAN HIDE IN THE CELLAR!
LET'S PRETEND WE'VE BEEN THROWN INTO A ROYAL DUNGEON AND ARE TRYING TO ESCAPE!

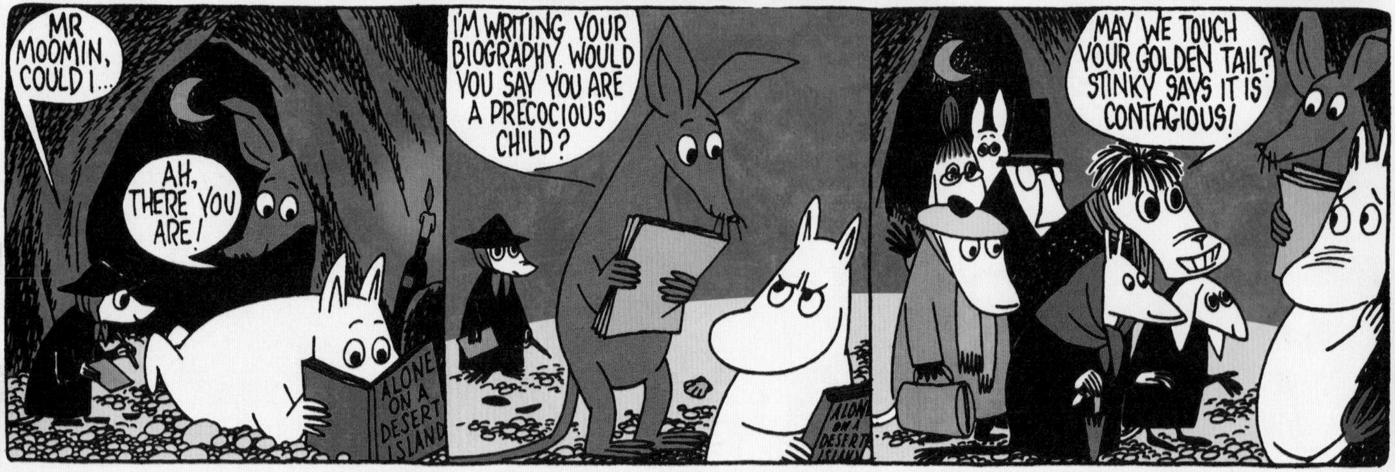
MR MOOMIN, COULD I...
AH, THERE YOU ARE!
ALONE ON A DESERT ISLAND
I'M WRITING YOUR BIOGRAPHY. WOULD YOU SAY YOU ARE A PRECOCIOUS CHILD?
MAY WE TOUCH YOUR GOLDEN TAIL? STINKY SAYS IT IS CONTAGIOUS!

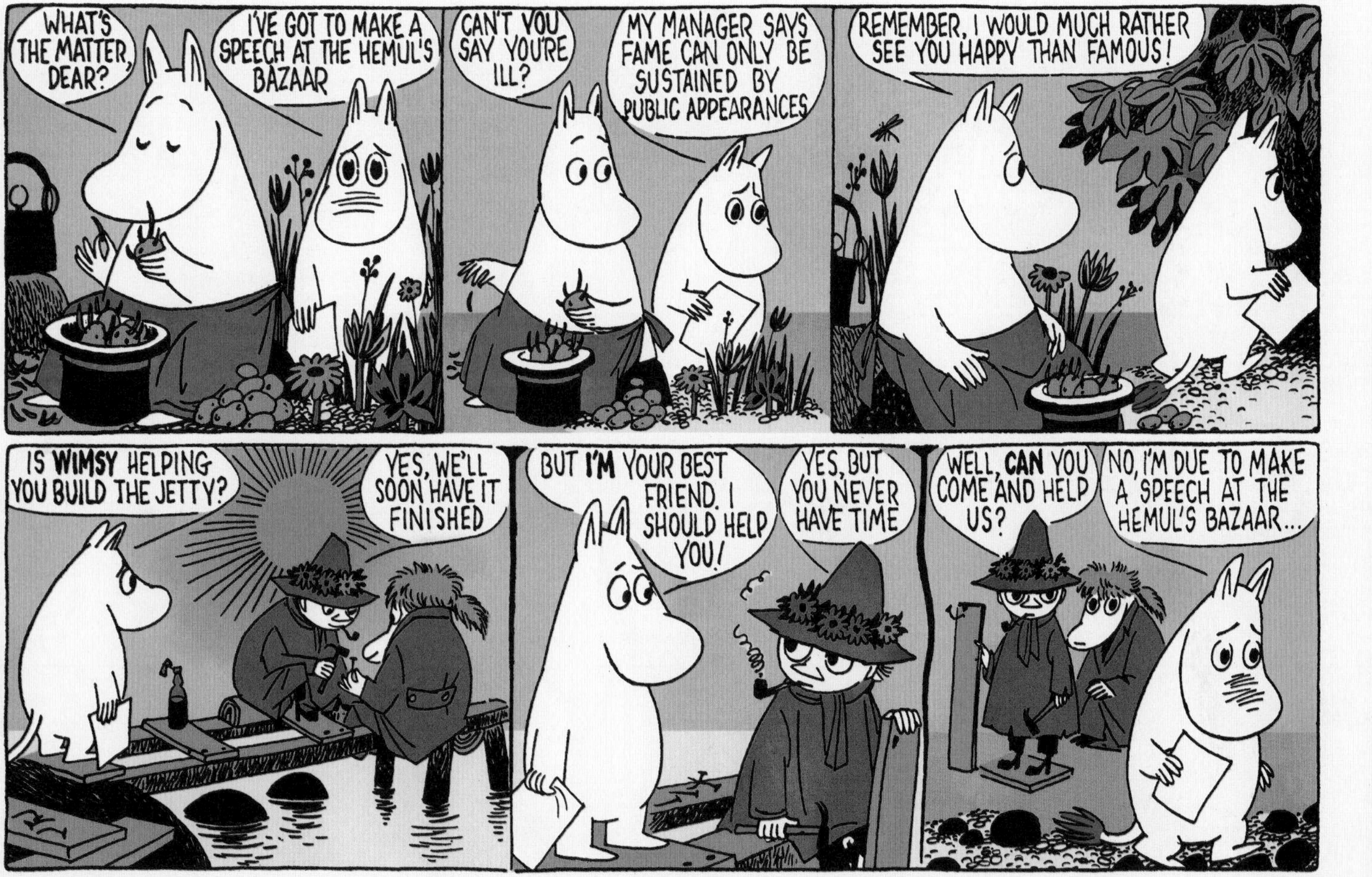
WHAT'S THE MATTER, DEAR?
I'VE GOT TO MAKE A SPEECH AT THE HEMUL'S BAZAAR
CAN'T YOU SAY YOU'RE ILL?
MY MANAGER SAYS FAME CAN ONLY BE SUSTAINED BY PUBLIC APPEARANCES
REMEMBER, I WOULD MUCH RATHER SEE YOU HAPPY THAN FAMOUS!
IS WIMSY HELPING YOU BUILD THE JETTY?
YES, WE'LL SOON HAVE IT FINISHED
BUT I'M YOUR BEST FRIEND. I SHOULD HELP YOU!
YES, BUT YOU NEVER HAVE TIME
WELL, CAN YOU COME AND HELP US?
NO, I'M DUE TO MAKE A SPEECH AT THE HEMUL'S BAZAAR...

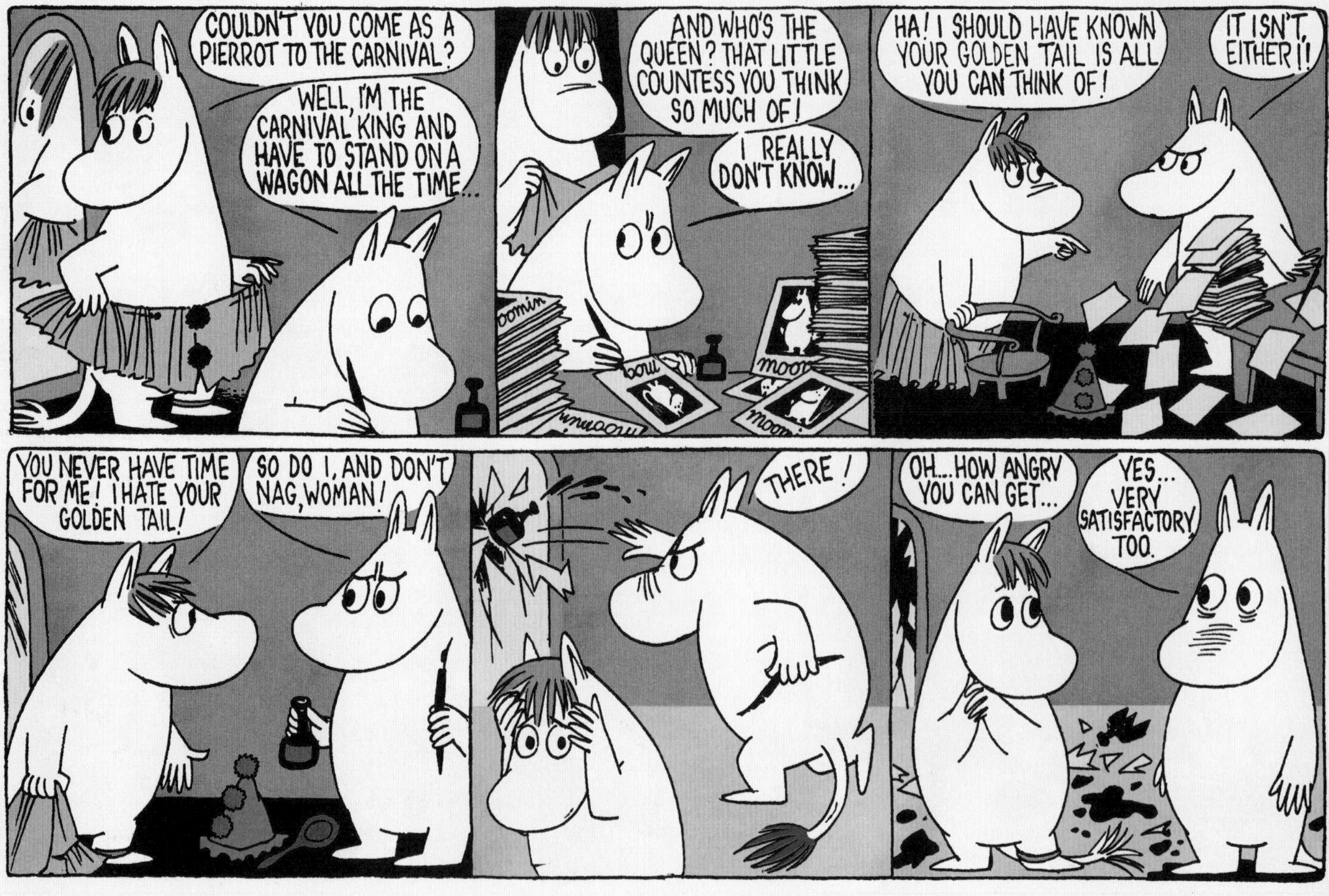
COULDN'T YOU COME AS A PIERROT TO THE CARNIVAL?
WELL, I'M THE CARNIVAL KING AND HAVE TO STAND ON A WAGON ALL THE TIME...
AND WHO'S THE QUEEN? THAT LITTLE COUNTESS YOU THINK SO MUCH OF!
I REALLY DON'T KNOW...
HA! I SHOULD HAVE KNOWN YOUR GOLDEN TAIL IS ALL YOU CAN THINK OF!
IT ISN'T, EITHER!!
YOU NEVER HAVE TIME FOR ME! I HATE YOUR GOLDEN TAIL!
SO DO I, AND DON'T NAG, WOMAN!
THERE!
OH... HOW ANGRY YOU CAN GET...
YES... VERY SATISFACTORY TOO.

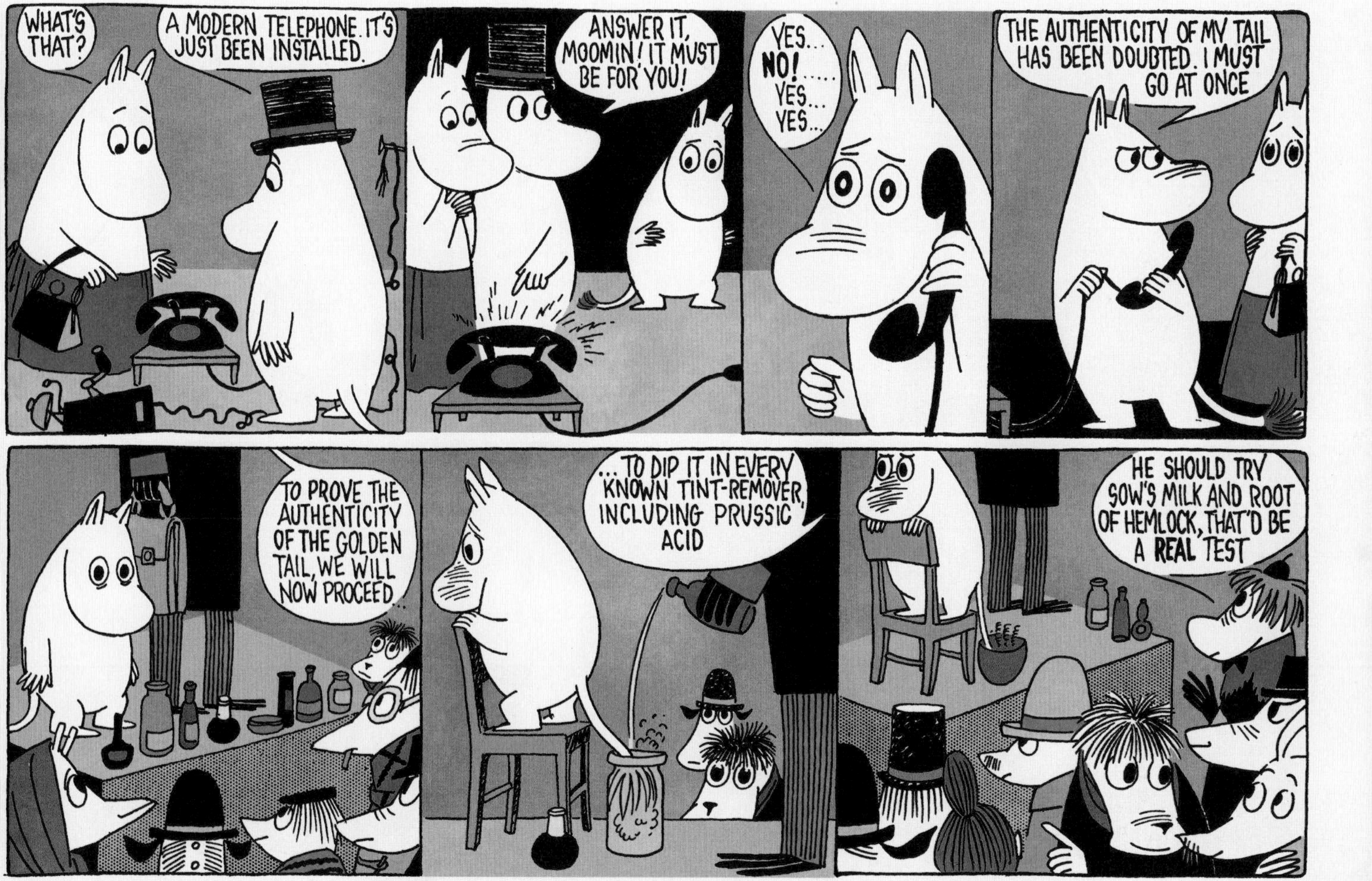
WHAT'S THAT?
A MODERN TELEPHONE. IT'S JUST BEEN INSTALLED.
ANSWER IT, MOOMIN! IT MUST BE FOR YOU!
YES... NO!..... YES... YES...
THE AUTHENTICITY OF MY TAIL HAS BEEN DOUBTED. I MUST GO AT ONCE
TO PROVE THE AUTHENTICITY OF THE GOLDEN TAIL, WE WILL NOW PROCEED...
...TO DIP IT IN EVERY KNOWN TINT-REMOVER, INCLUDING PRUSSIC ACID
HE SHOULD TRY SOW'S MILK AND ROOT OF HEMLOCK, THAT'D BE A REAL TEST

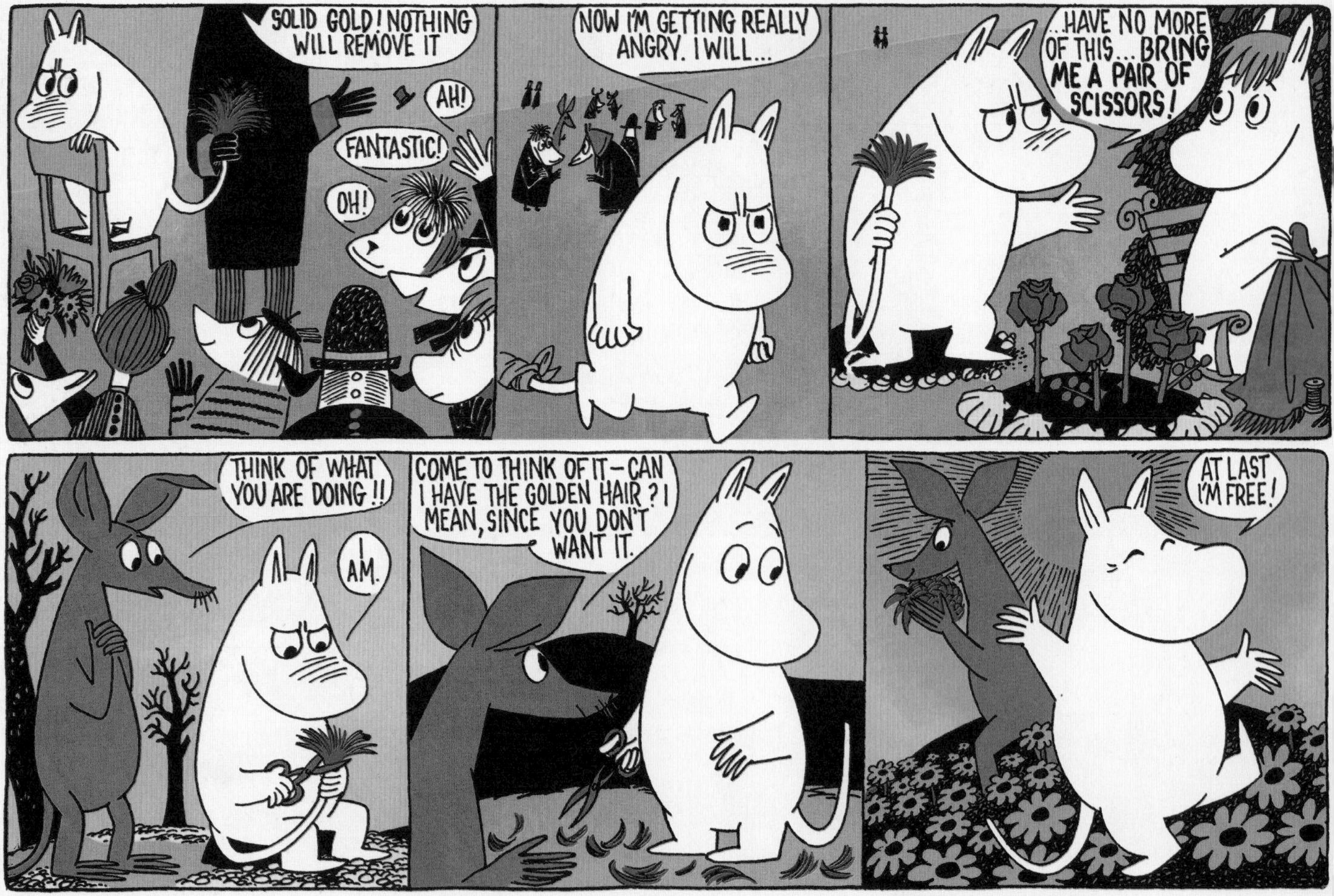
SOLID GOLD! NOTHING WILL REMOVE IT
AH!
FANTASTIC!
OH!
NOW I'M GETTING REALLY ANGRY. I WILL...
...HAVE NO MORE OF THIS... BRING ME A PAIR OF SCISSORS!
THINK OF WHAT YOU ARE DOING!!
I AM.
COME TO THINK OF IT—CAN I HAVE THE GOLDEN HAIR? I MEAN, SINCE YOU DON'T WANT IT.
AT LAST I'M FREE!

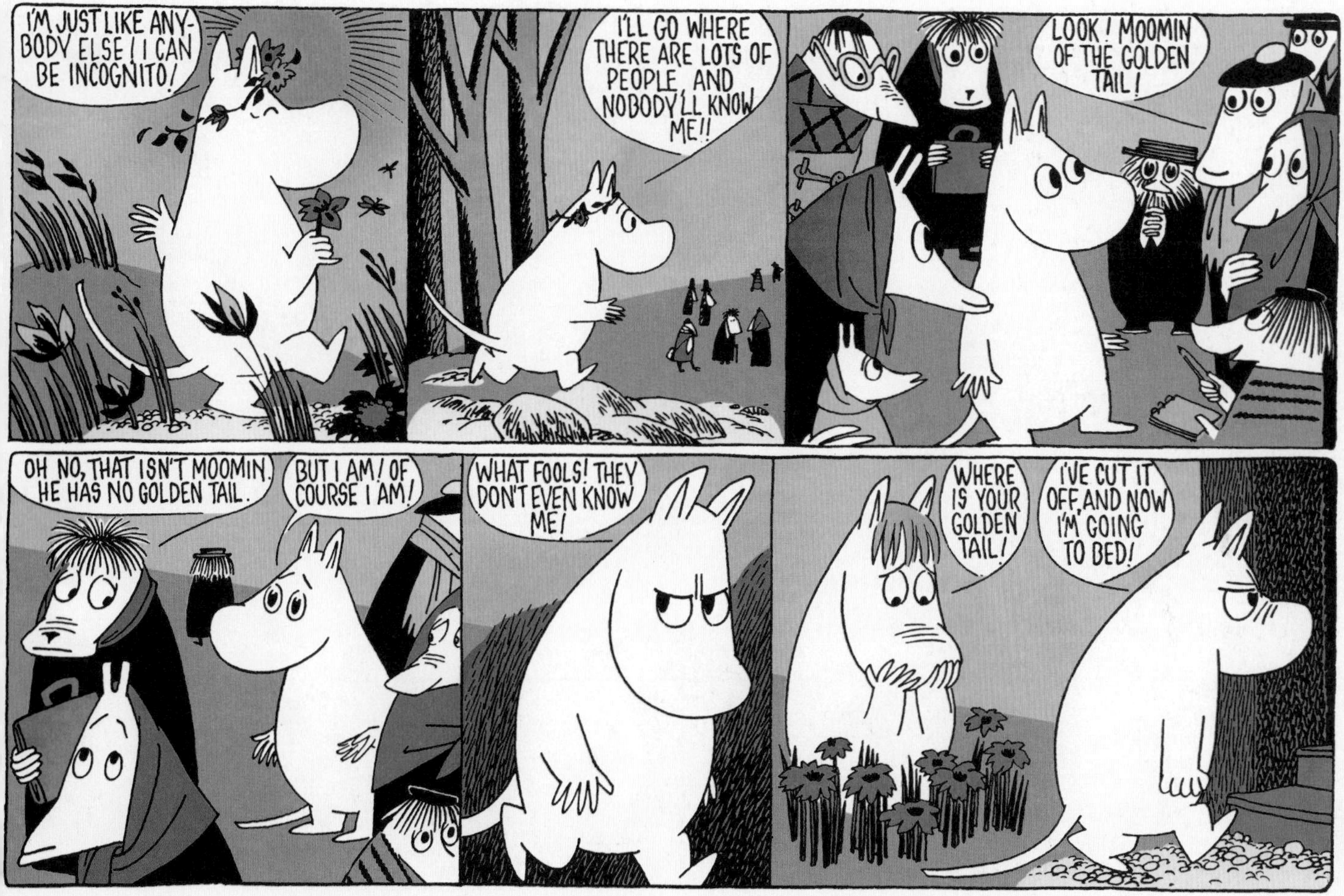
I'M JUST LIKE ANYBODY ELSE! I CAN BE INCOGNITO!
I'LL GO WHERE THERE ARE LOTS OF PEOPLE, AND NOBODY'LL KNOW ME!!
LOOK! MOOMIN OF THE GOLDEN TAIL!
OH NO, THAT ISN'T MOOMIN. HE HAS NO GOLDEN TAIL.
BUT I AM! OF COURSE I AM!
WHAT FOOLS! THEY DON'T EVEN KNOW ME!
WHERE IS YOUR GOLDEN TAIL!
I'VE CUT IT OFF, AND NOW I'M GOING TO BED!

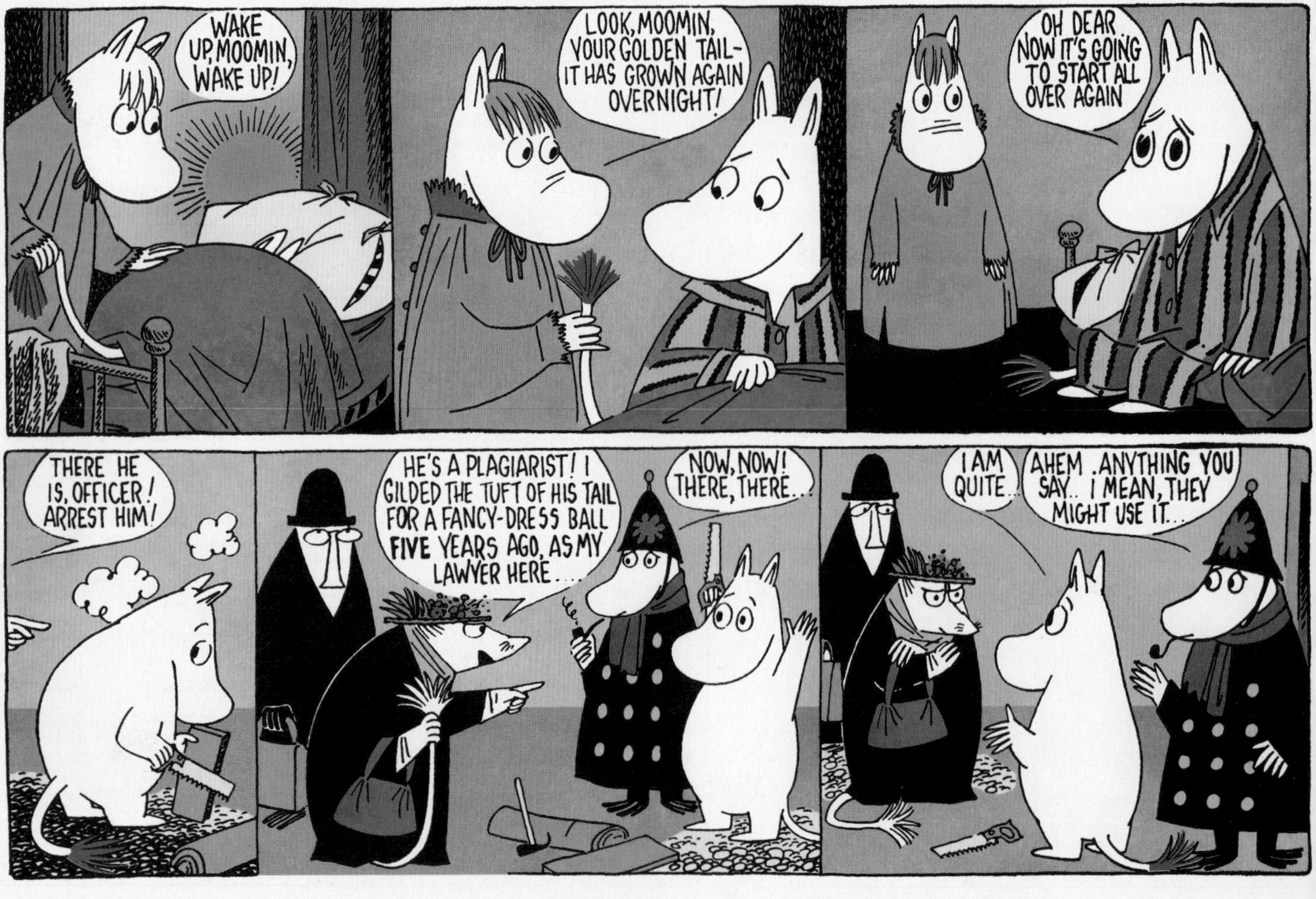
WAKE UP, MOOMIN, WAKE UP!
LOOK, MOOMIN, YOUR GOLDEN TAIL- IT HAS GROWN AGAIN OVERNIGHT!
OH DEAR. NOW IT'S GOING TO START ALL OVER AGAIN
THERE HE IS, OFFICER! ARREST HIM!
HE'S A PLAGIARIST! I GILDED THE TUFT OF HIS TAIL FOR A FANCY-DRESS BALL **FIVE** YEARS AGO, AS MY LAWYER HERE....
NOW, NOW! THERE, THERE...
I AM QUITE..
AHEM. ANYTHING YOU SAY.. I MEAN, THEY MIGHT USE IT...

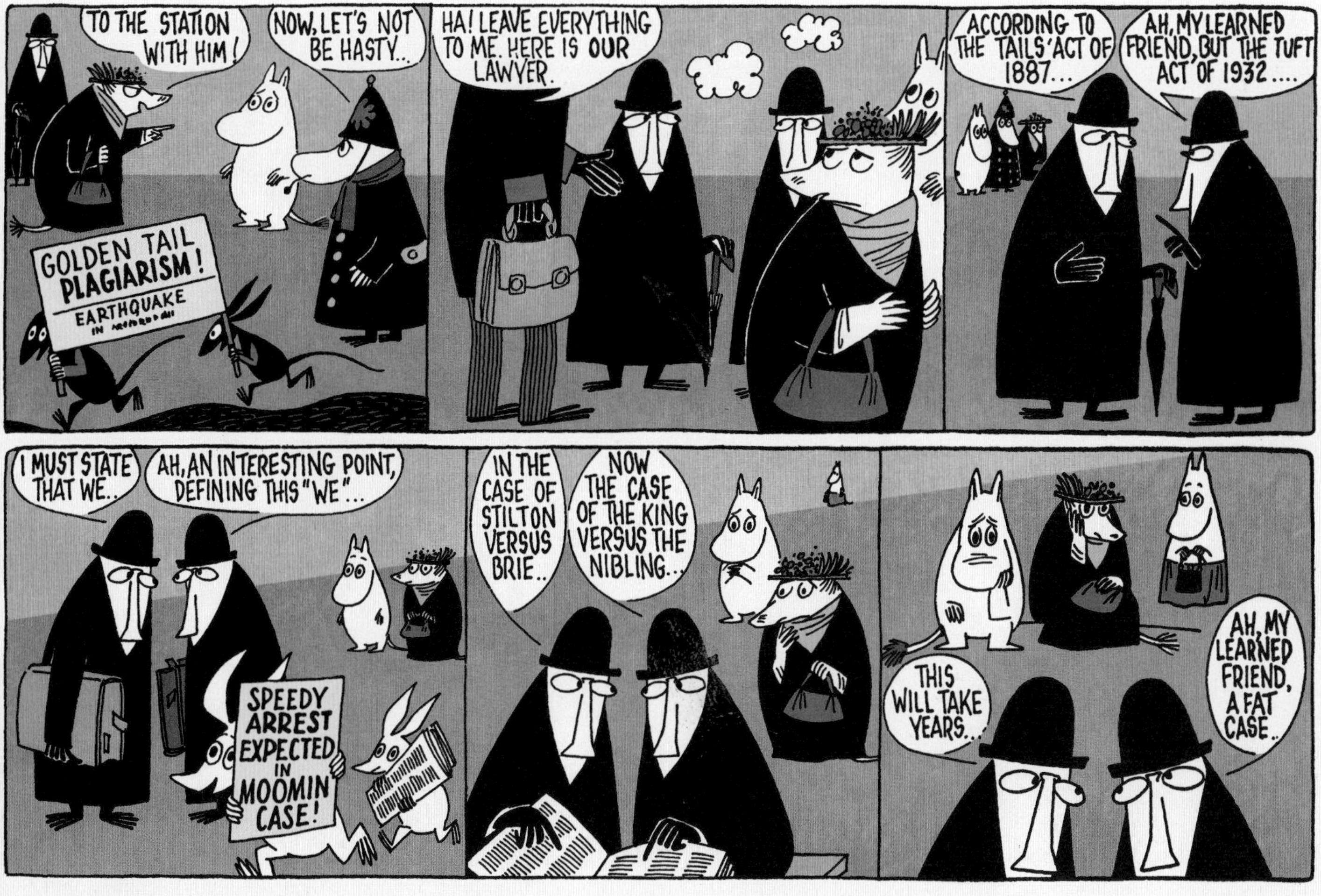

TO THE STATION WITH HIM!
NOW, LET'S NOT BE HASTY...
GOLDEN TAIL PLAGIARISM!
EARTHQUAKE
HA! LEAVE EVERYTHING TO ME. HERE IS OUR LAWYER.
ACCORDING TO THE TAILS' ACT OF 1887...
AH, MY LEARNED FRIEND, BUT THE TUFT ACT OF 1932....
I MUST STATE THAT WE..
AH, AN INTERESTING POINT, DEFINING THIS "WE"...
SPEEDY ARREST EXPECTED IN MOOMIN CASE!
IN THE CASE OF STILTON VERSUS BRIE..
NOW THE CASE OF THE KING VERSUS THE NIBLING...
THIS WILL TAKE YEARS...
AH, MY LEARNED FRIEND, A FAT CASE..

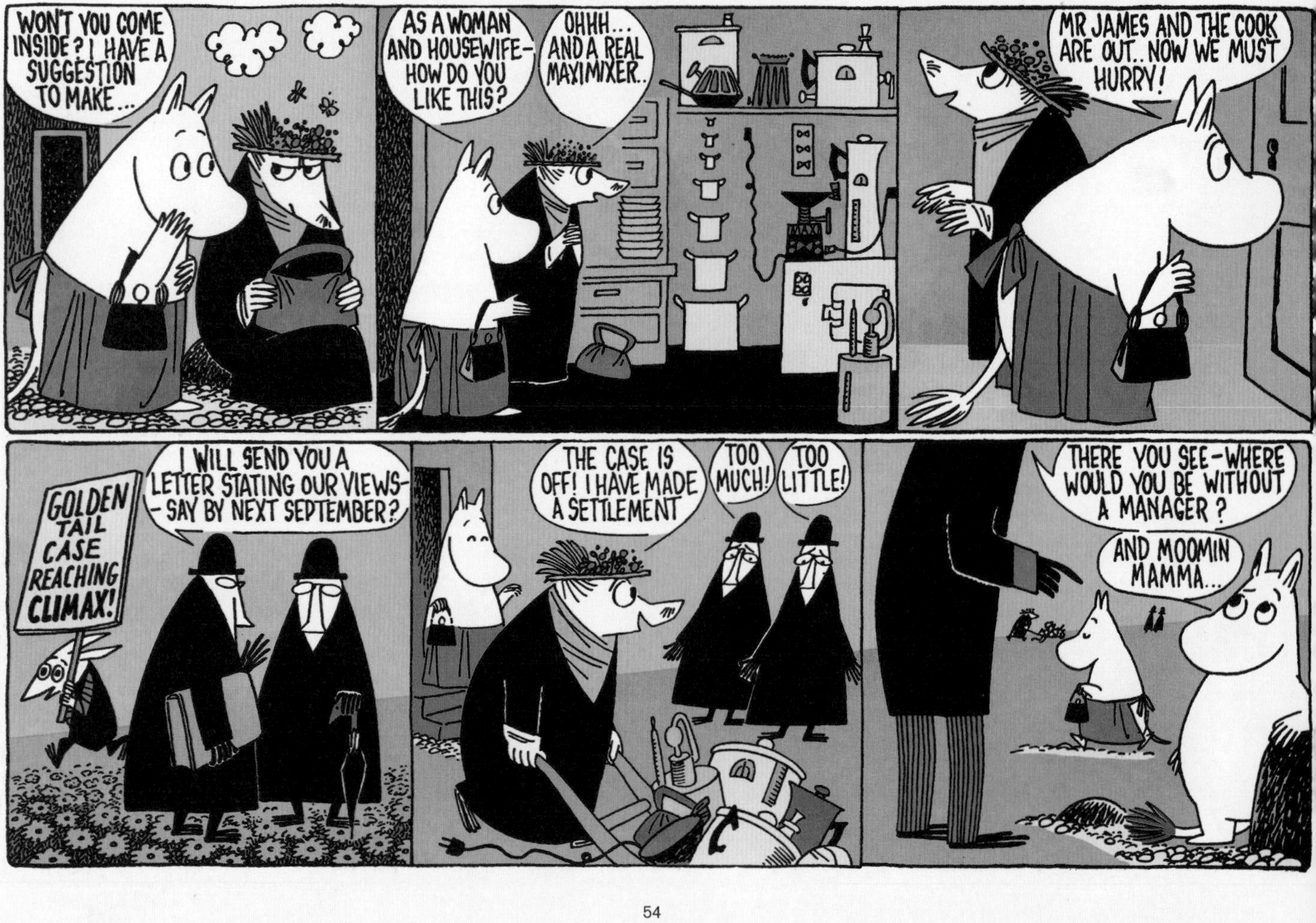
WON'T YOU COME INSIDE? I HAVE A SUGGESTION TO MAKE...
AS A WOMAN AND HOUSEWIFE - HOW DO YOU LIKE THIS?
OHHH... AND A REAL MAXIMIXER..
MR JAMES AND THE COOK ARE OUT.. NOW WE MUST HURRY!
GOLDEN TAIL CASE REACHING CLIMAX!
I WILL SEND YOU A LETTER STATING OUR VIEWS - SAY BY NEXT SEPTEMBER?
THE CASE IS OFF! I HAVE MADE A SETTLEMENT
TOO MUCH!
TOO LITTLE!
THERE YOU SEE - WHERE WOULD YOU BE WITHOUT A MANAGER?
AND MOOMIN MAMMA...

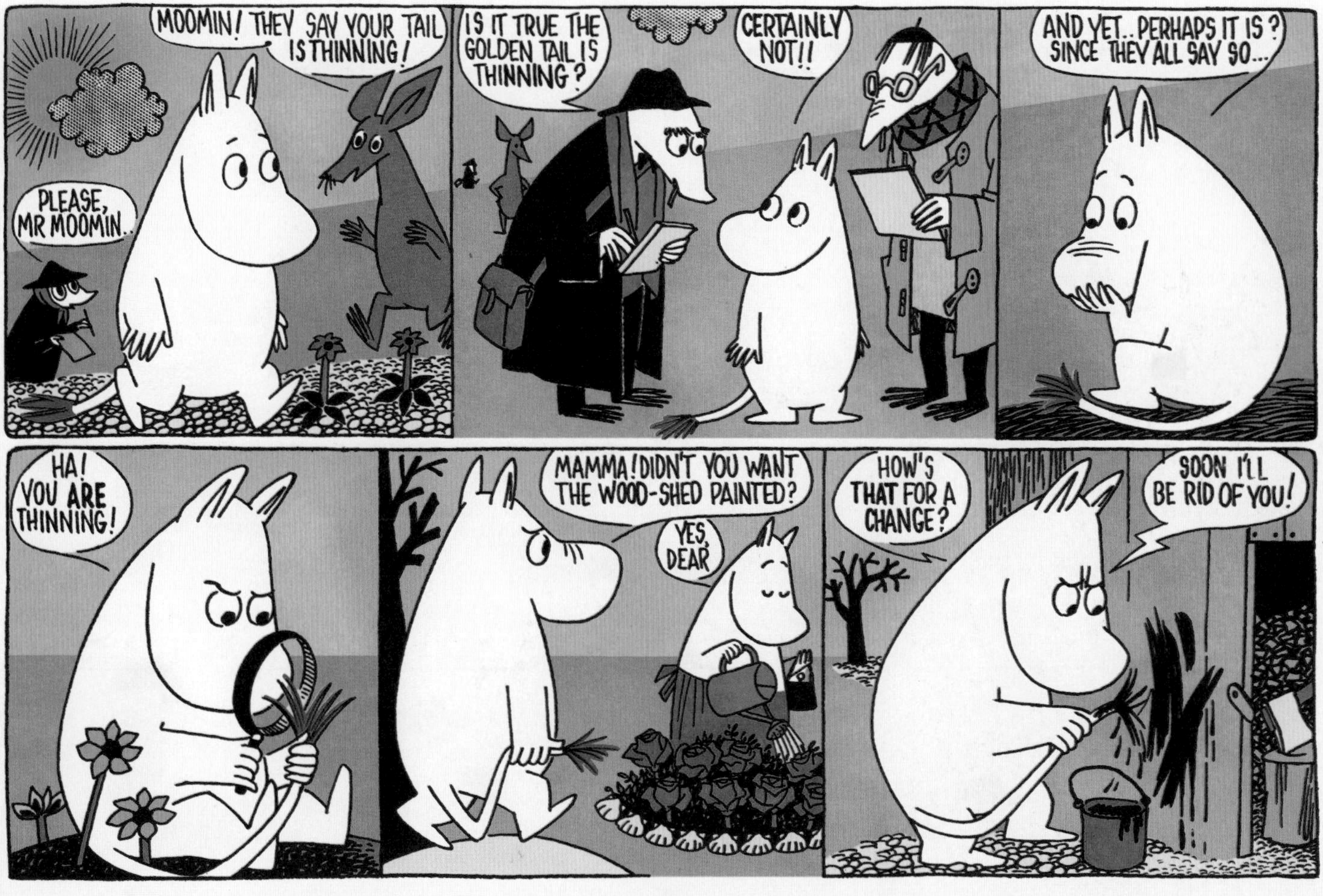
MOOMIN! THEY SAY YOUR TAIL IS THINNING!
PLEASE, MR MOOMIN..
IS IT TRUE THE GOLDEN TAIL IS THINNING?
CERTAINLY NOT!!
AND YET.. PERHAPS IT IS? SINCE THEY ALL SAY SO...
HA! YOU **ARE** THINNING!
MAMMA! DIDN'T YOU WANT THE WOOD-SHED PAINTED?
YES, DEAR
HOW'S THAT FOR A CHANGE?
SOON I'LL BE RID OF YOU!

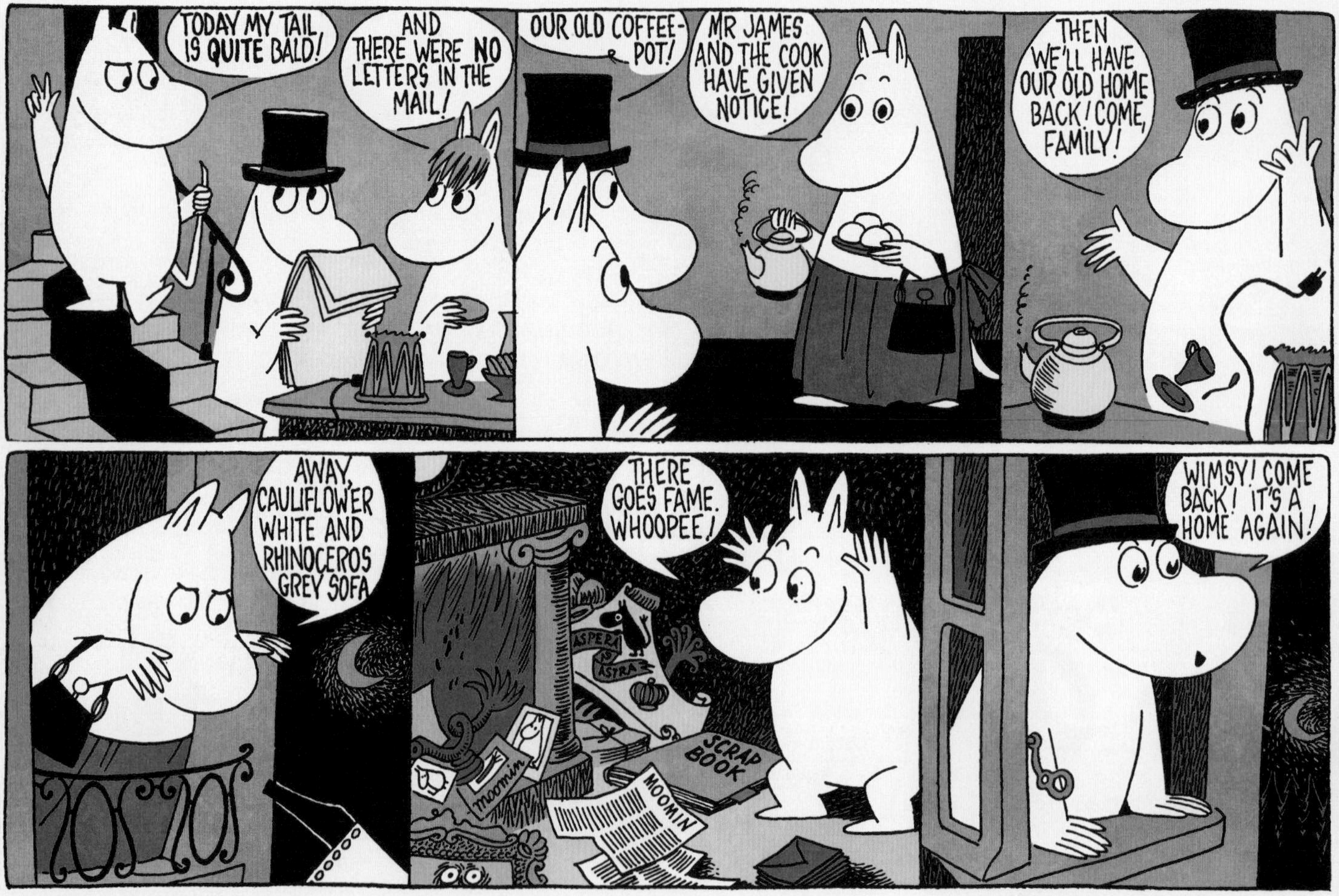
TODAY MY TAIL IS **QUITE** BALD!
AND THERE WERE **NO** LETTERS IN THE MAIL!
OUR OLD COFFEE-POT!
MR JAMES AND THE COOK HAVE GIVEN NOTICE!
THEN WE'LL HAVE OUR OLD HOME BACK! COME, FAMILY!
AWAY, CAULIFLOWER WHITE AND RHINOCEROS GREY SOFA
ASPERA AD ASTRA
THERE GOES FAME. WHOOPEE!
SCRAP BOOK
MOOMIN
moomin
WIMSY! COME BACK! IT'S A HOME AGAIN!

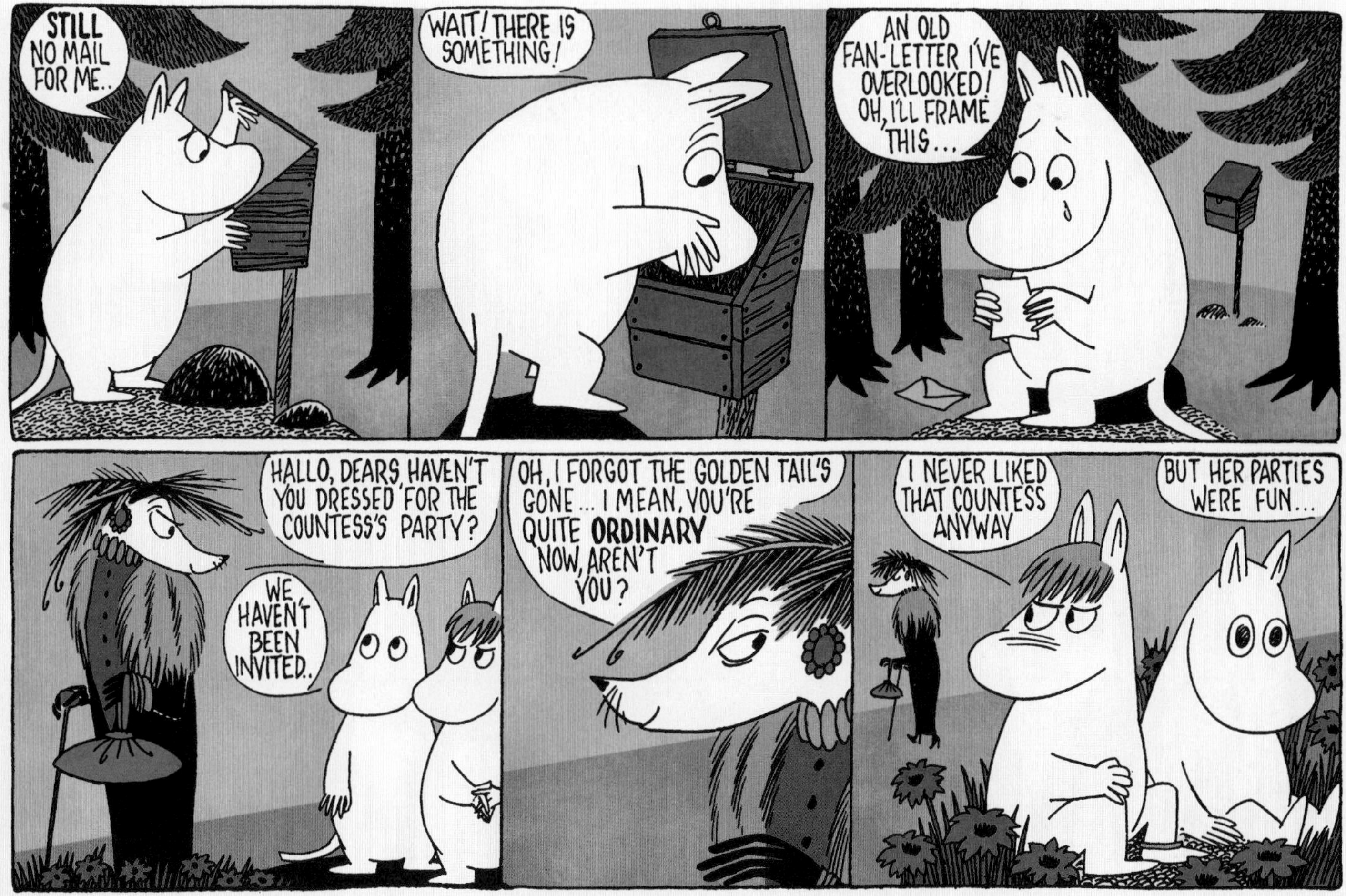
STILL NO MAIL FOR ME..
WAIT! THERE IS SOMETHING!
AN OLD FAN-LETTER I'VE OVERLOOKED! OH, I'LL FRAME THIS...
HALLO, DEARS HAVEN'T YOU DRESSED FOR THE COUNTESS'S PARTY?
WE HAVEN'T BEEN INVITED..
OH, I FORGOT THE GOLDEN TAIL'S GONE ... I MEAN, YOU'RE QUITE **ORDINARY** NOW, AREN'T YOU?
I NEVER LIKED THAT COUNTESS ANYWAY
BUT HER PARTIES WERE FUN...

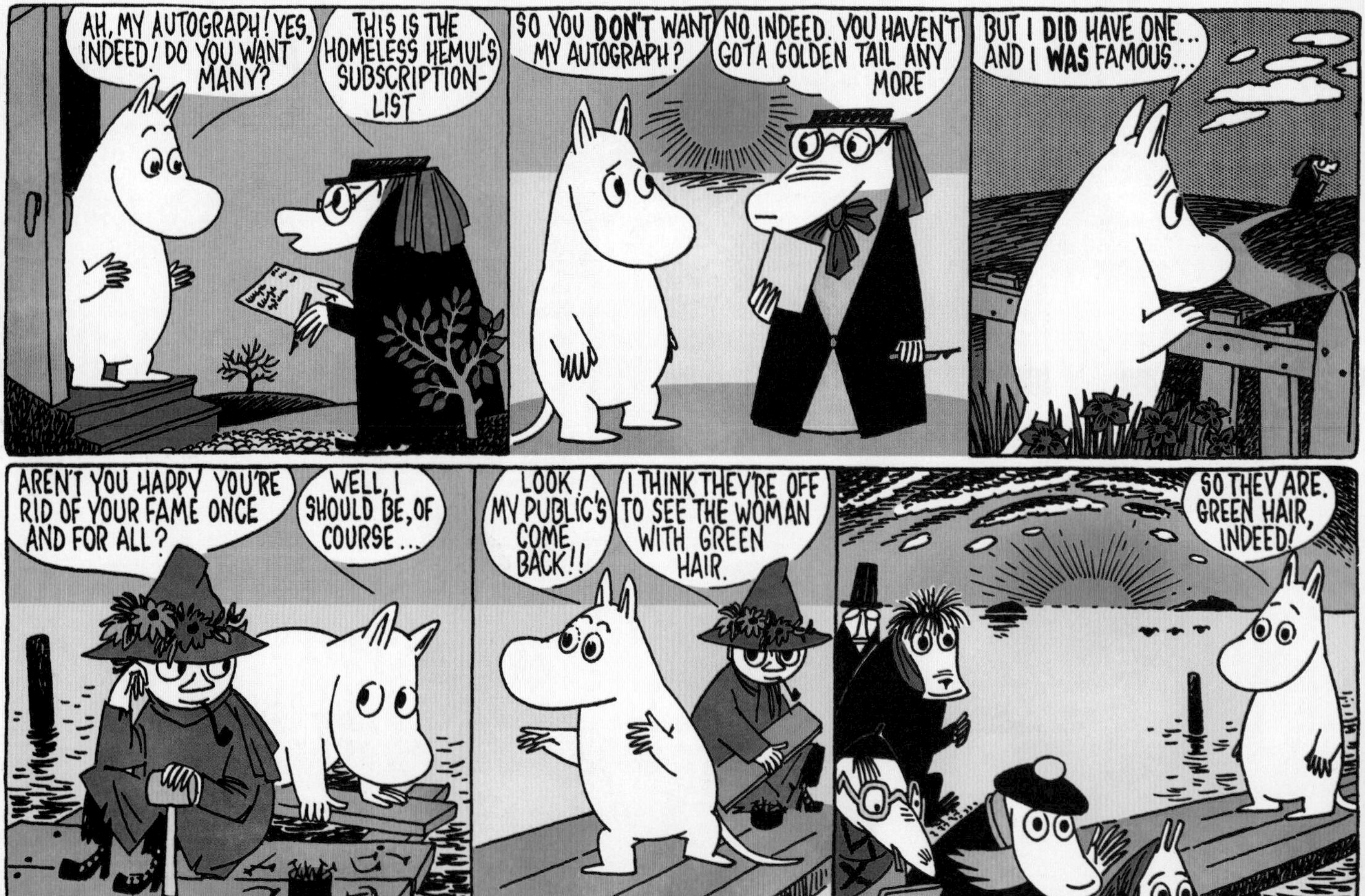
AH, MY AUTOGRAPH! YES, INDEED! DO YOU WANT MANY?
THIS IS THE HOMELESS HEMUL'S SUBSCRIPTION-LIST
SO YOU DON'T WANT MY AUTOGRAPH?
NO, INDEED. YOU HAVEN'T GOT A GOLDEN TAIL ANY MORE
BUT I DID HAVE ONE... AND I WAS FAMOUS...
AREN'T YOU HAPPY YOU'RE RID OF YOUR FAME ONCE AND FOR ALL?
WELL, I SHOULD BE, OF COURSE...
LOOK! MY PUBLIC'S COME BACK!!
I THINK THEY'RE OFF TO SEE THE WOMAN WITH GREEN HAIR.
SO THEY ARE. GREEN HAIR, INDEED!

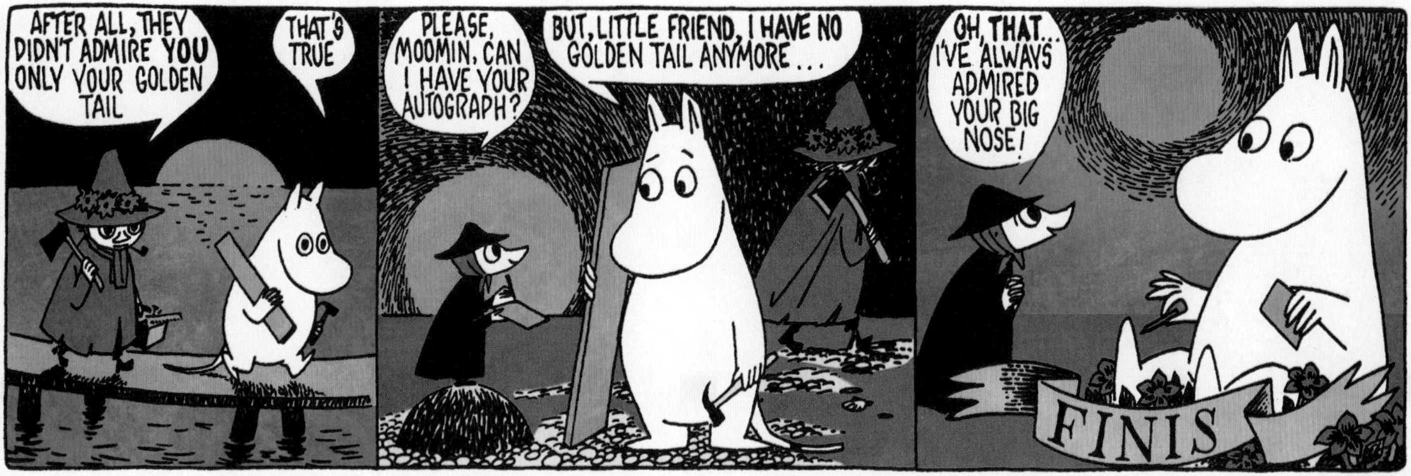
AFTER ALL, THEY DIDN'T ADMIRE **YOU** ONLY YOUR GOLDEN TAIL
THAT'S TRUE
PLEASE, MOOMIN, CAN I HAVE YOUR AUTOGRAPH?
BUT, LITTLE FRIEND, I HAVE NO GOLDEN TAIL ANYMORE . . .
OH, **THAT**... I'VE "ALWAYS" ADMIRED YOUR BIG NOSE!
FINIS

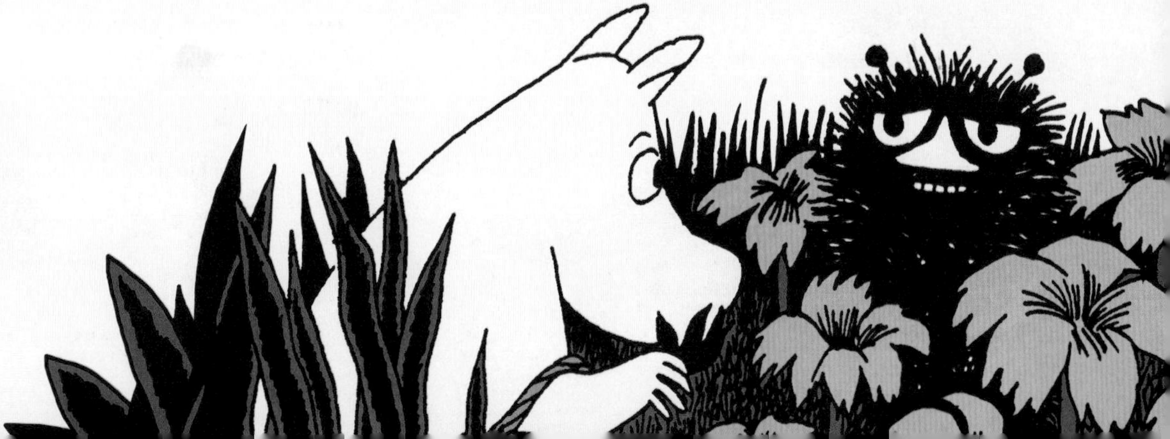

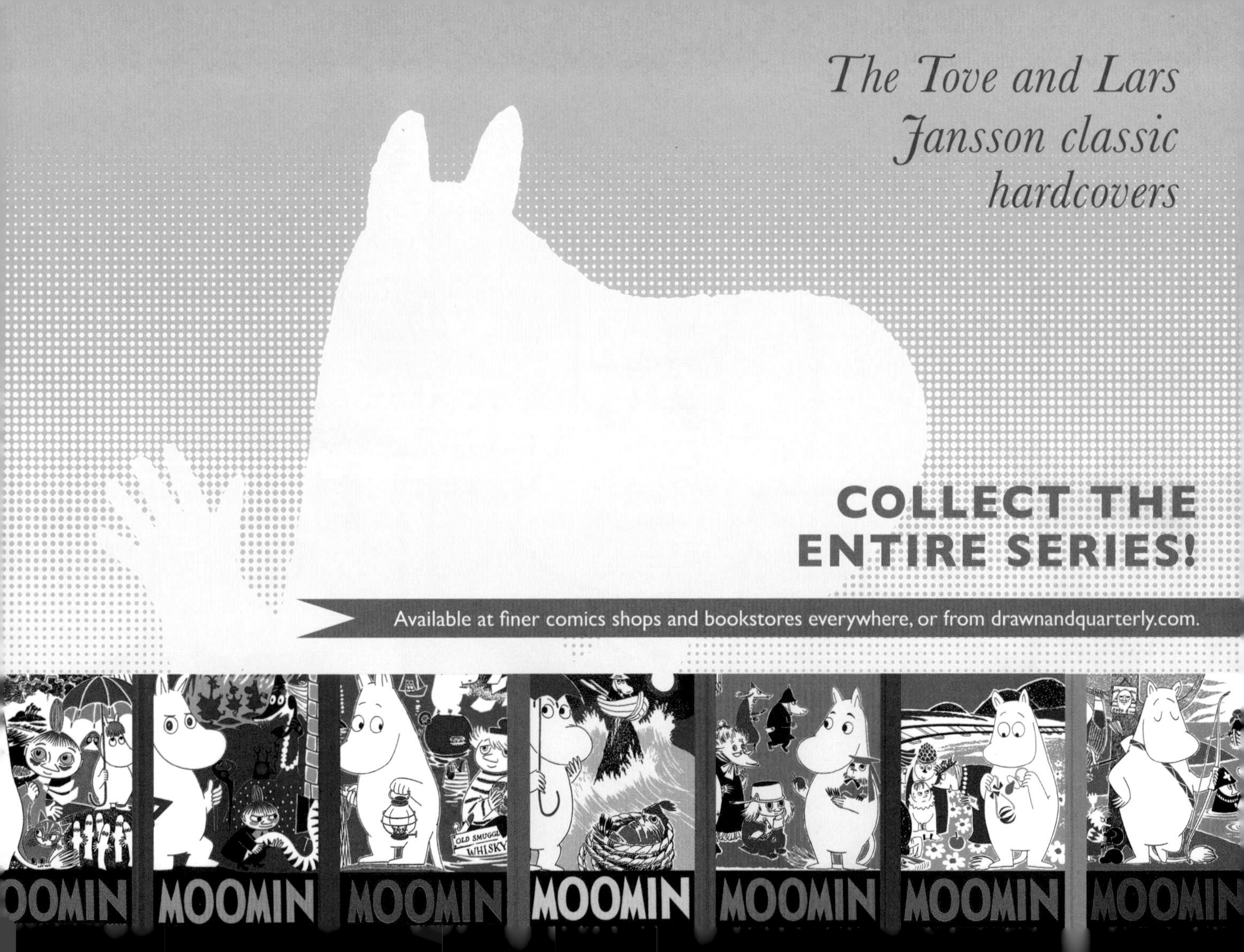
OOMIN
MOOMIN
MOOMIN
WHISKY
MOOMIN
MOOMIN
MOOMIN
MOOMIN

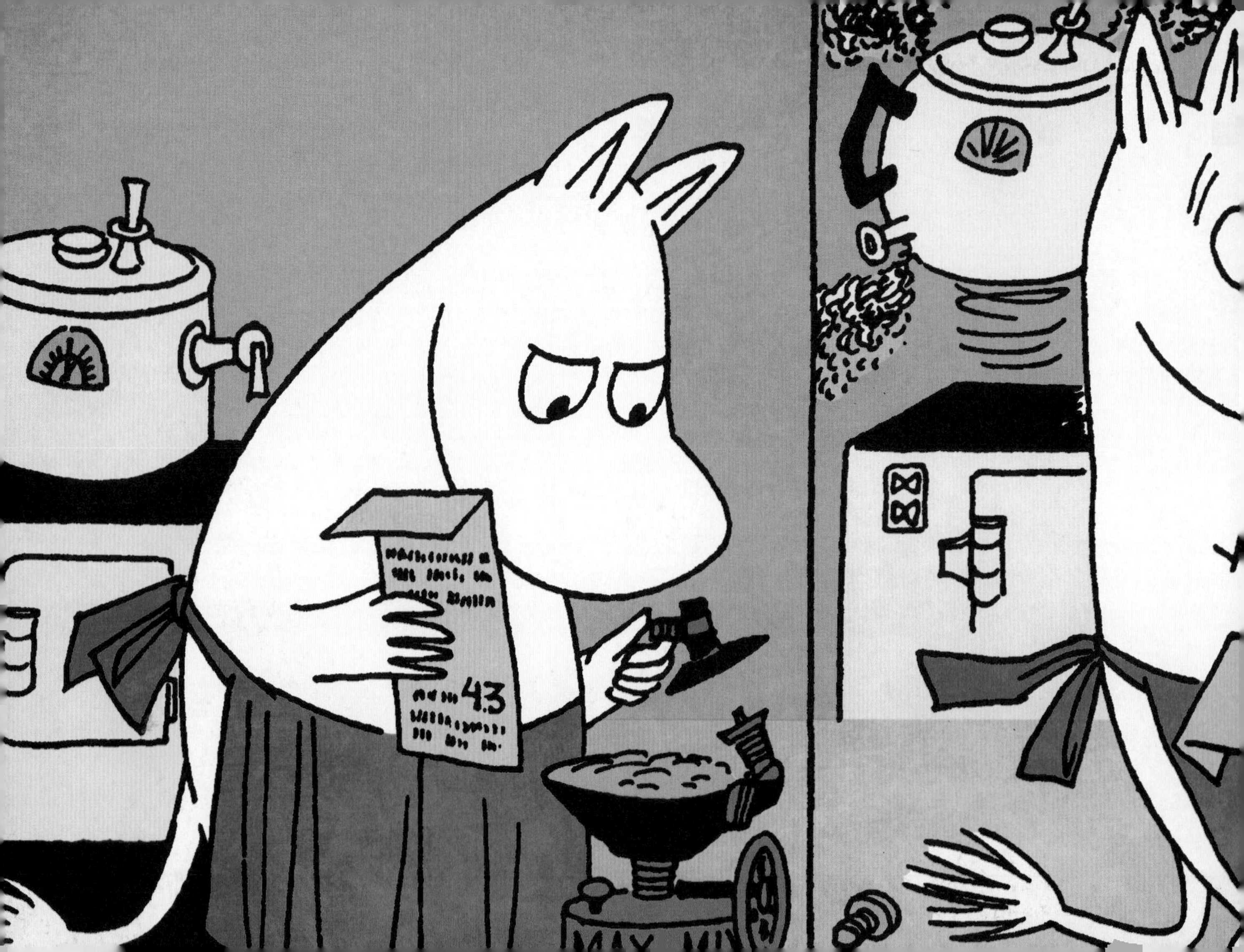
43
MAX

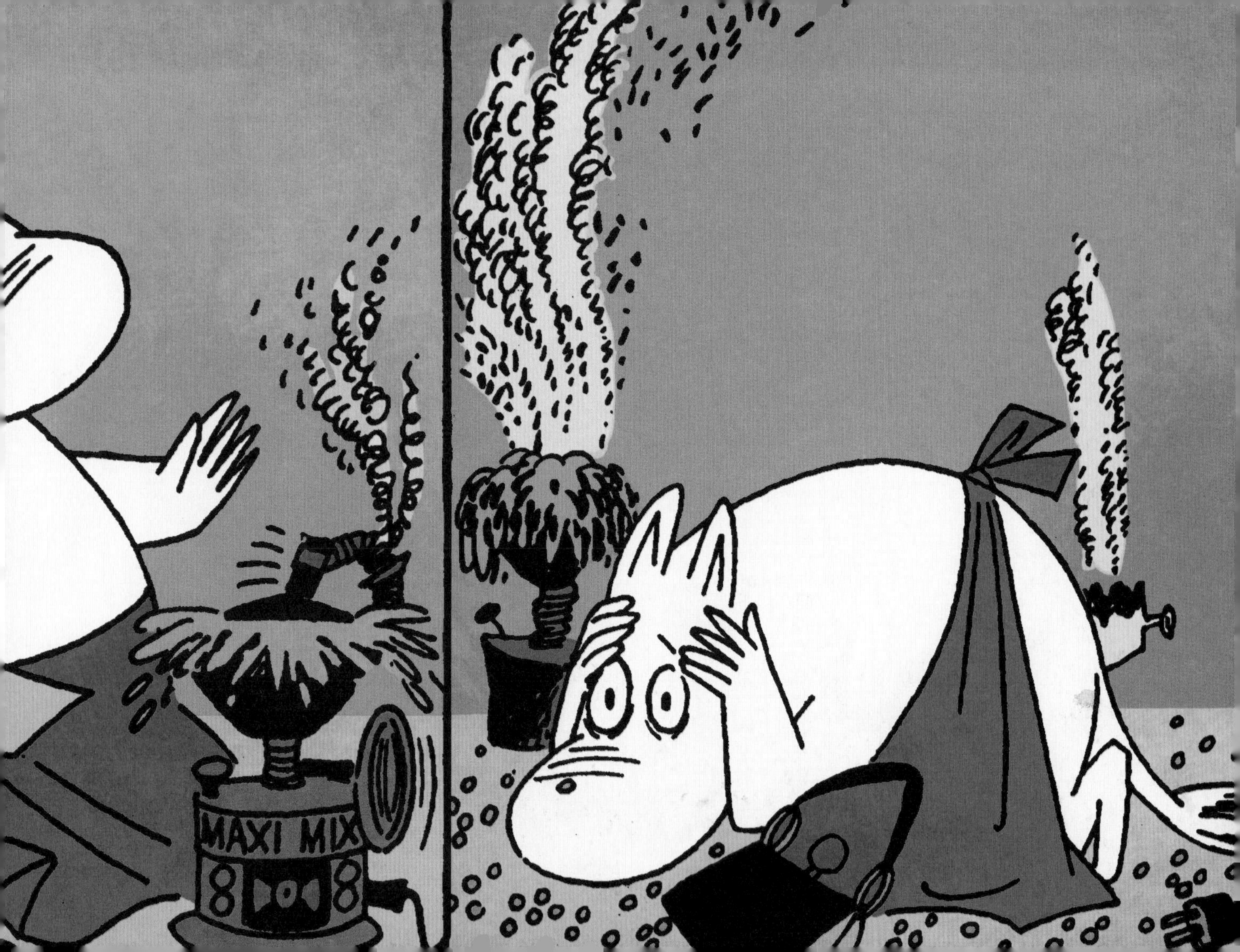
MAXI MIX

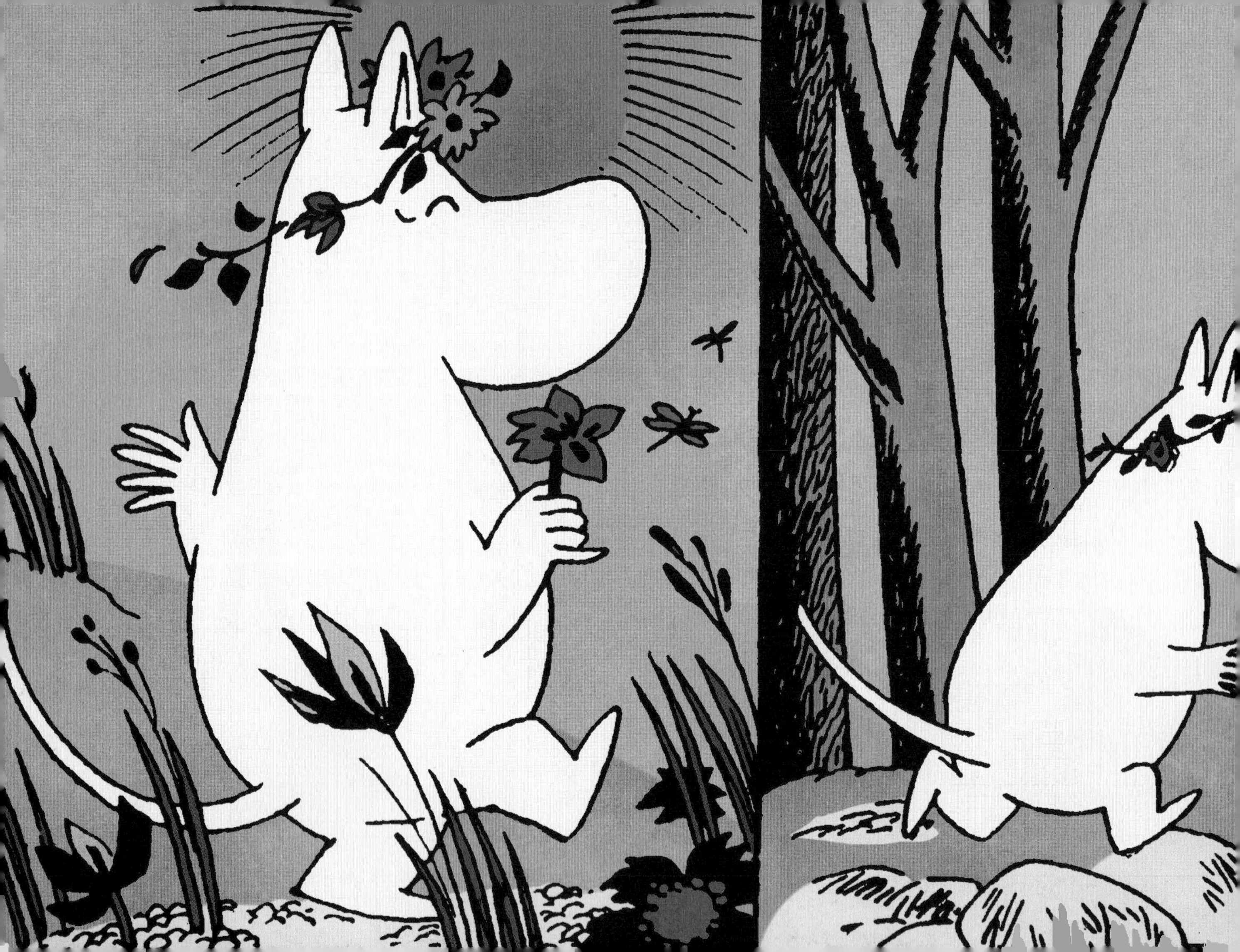

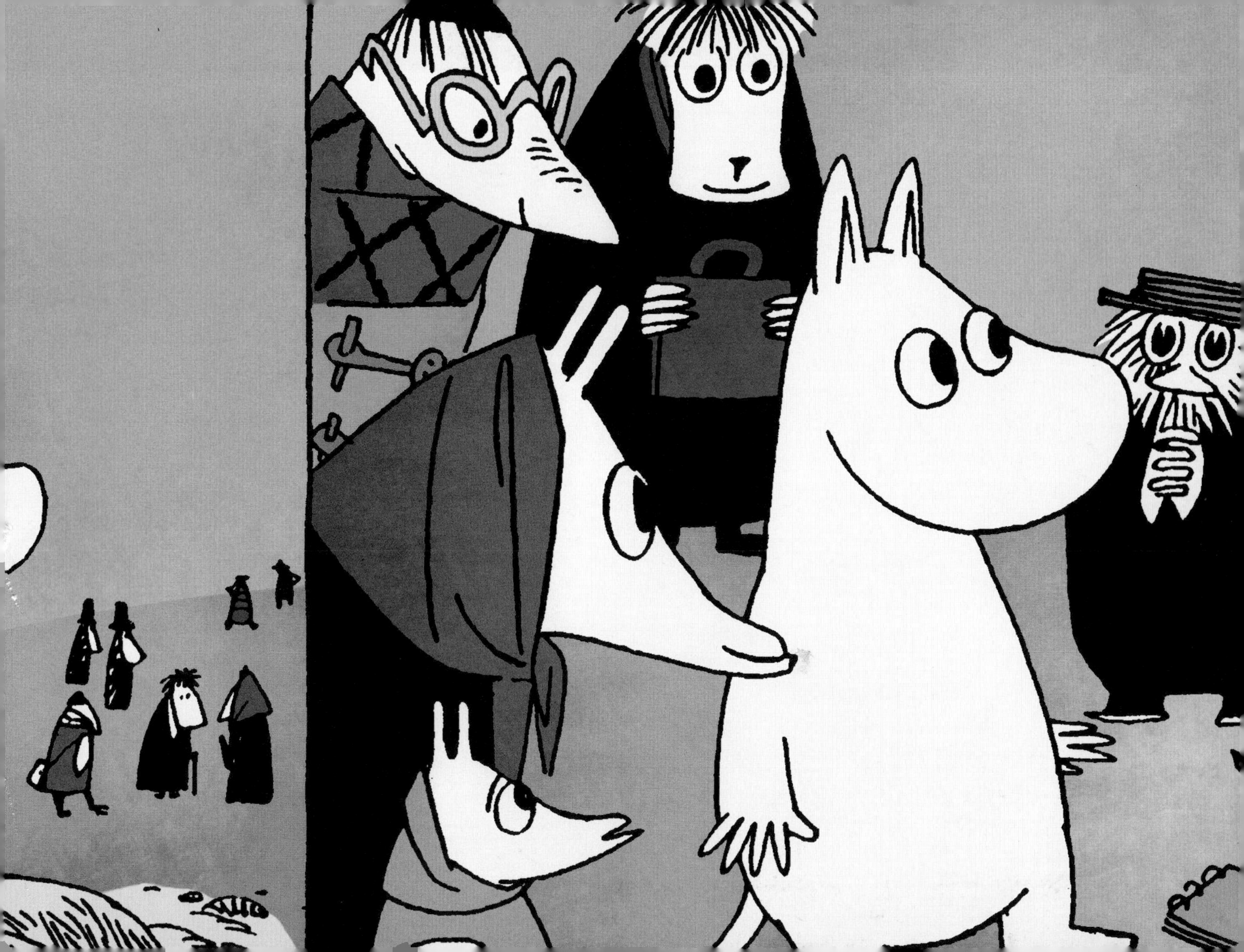

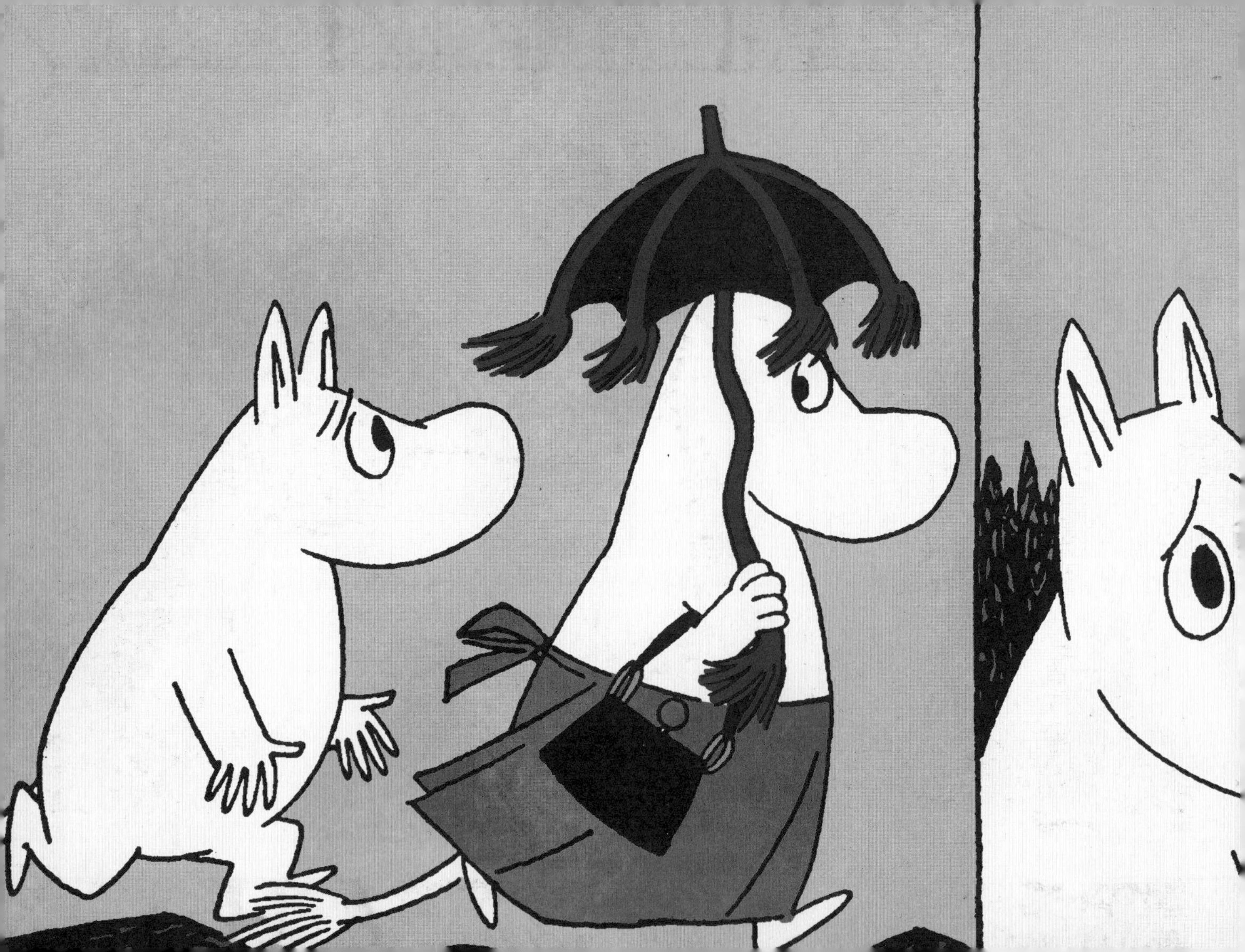